A Season of Gifts

Also by Richard Peck

RICHARD PECK

A Season of Gifts

DIAL BOOKS FOR YOUNG READERS

DIAL BOOKS FOR YOUNG READERS
A division of Penguin Young Readers Group
Published by The Penguin Group
Penguin Group (USA) Inc., 375 Hudson Street, New York, NY 10014, U.S.A.
Penguin Group (Canada), 90 Eglinton Avenue East, Suite 700, Toronto, Ontario,
Canada M4P 2Y3 (a division of Pearson Penguin Canada Inc.) • Penguin Books
Ltd, 80 Strand, London WC2R 0RL, England • Penguin Ireland, 25 St. Stephen's
Green, Dublin 2, Ireland (a division of Penguin Books Ltd) • Penguin Group
(Australia), 250 Camberwell Road, Camberwell, Victoria 3124, Australia (a
division of Pearson Australia Group Pty Ltd) • Penguin Books India Pvt Ltd,
11 Community Centre, Panchsheel Park, New Delhi - 110 017, India • Penguin
Group (NZ), 67 Apollo Drive, Rosedale, North Shore 0632, New Zealand (a
division of Pearson New Zealand Ltd) • Penguin Books (South Africa) (Pty) Ltd,
24 Sturdee Avenue, Rosebank, Johannesburg 2196, South Africa • Penguin Books
Ltd, Registered Offices: 80 Strand, London WC2R 0RL, England

Designed by Jennifer Kelly • Text set in Centaur
Printed in the U.S.A.

1 3 5 7 9 10 8 6 4 2

Peck, Richard, date.
A season of gifts / Richard Peck.
p. cm.
A companion novel to A long way from Chicago and A year down yonder.
Summary: Relates the surprising gifts bestowed on twelve-year-old Bob Barnhart
and his family, who have recently moved to a small Illinois town in 1958,
by their larger-than-life neighbor, Mrs. Dowdel.
ISBN 978-0-8037-3082-3
[1. Neighbors—Fiction. 2. Moving, Household—Fiction. 3. Illinois—
History—20th century—Fiction. 4. Humorous stories.] I. Title.
PZ7.P338Sd 2009
[Fic]—dc22
2008048050

for Maryann and George MacDonald

Contents

A Season of Gifts

The Last House
in Town

CHAPTER ONE

Locked and Loaded

You could see from here the house was haunted. Its crooked old lightning rods pointed bony fingers at the sky. It hadn't had a lick of paint since VJ Day, maybe the war before that. A porch sagged off the side. The kitchen screen door hung from a hinge. Only the snowball bushes crowding its foundations seemed to hold the place up.

At night, lights moved from room to room. Every evening just at dusk a light bobbed down the walk to the cobhouse and the privy behind, and back again.

My little sister, Ruth Ann, couldn't take her eyes off the place. She'd rest her chin on the windowsill and plant her nose on screen wire. What else did she have to do?

"It's like Halloween here in August," she'd say. "I betcha there are spooks inside that house."

"No," Mother said behind her. "No spooks."

"What do you think, Bobby?" I was Ruth Ann's big brother, so she thought I knew things. "Spooks or not?"

Over her head, Mother gave me one of her direct looks, so I said, "Probably not."

But even when Ruth Ann took her hula hoop and her doll buggy out on our front walk, she was all eyes. She'd watch the house while she revolved in her hoop and rocked her doll. She spent a lot of time outside, hoping a friend would happen to her.

So we Barnharts had moved in next door to a haunted house, if a house can be haunted by a living being. But the old lady who lived over there had to be just this side of the grave with one foot in it. She looked older than the town. But she was way too solid to be a ghost. You sure couldn't see through her. You could barely see around her.

A long straight garden grew down this side of her property. Every blazing morning she'd tramp off her back porch and down her garden rows with a hoe humped on her shoulder. Her straw hat looked like she'd swiped it off a mule. It hid her face except for the chins. She worked right through high noon in a fog of flies, hoeing, yanking weeds, and talking to her tomato plants.

The heat slowed her some, and the flies. But she could be amazingly light on her big pins. We'd already seen her take a broom and swat a Fuller Brush man off her porch.

She kept right at his heels till he was off her property.

As everybody knew, she didn't neighbor and went to no known church. She was not only real cranky, but well-armed. Word was that she had a regular arsenal of weaponry behind her woodbox. They said it was like Fort Leonard Wood behind her stove. They said she was locked and loaded.

She had to be pushing ninety, so rumors had grown up around her. One was that her property was on top of an ancient Kickapoo burying grounds, and that's spooky right there.

Only a ragged row of fleshy red canna flowers separated her garden from our yard. "You children stay on this side of the cannas," Mother said. "Let's let sleeping dogs lie."

Mother didn't have to worry about me. I was a boy, but not that brave. I wouldn't have set a toe over that line. And she didn't mean my big sister, Phyllis, who was sulking upstairs over having to start high school in a new town. Mother meant Ruth Ann. She was hard to keep track of unless she was following you around.

"Remember who we are," Mother said. "And we're new here. All eyes are upon us."

It wasn't going to be the kind of town that rolls out the welcome mat. Still, a few people brought us things to eat just to see us up close. On a good day, an angel food cake. Moore's IGA store sent us out some half-price coupons and a sample size of Rinso soap. But Moore's was cash-and-carry, and we didn't have any cash.

Toward the end of our first week, somebody left five dandy ears of sweet corn on our porch. They were half silked to show the pearly kernels. But unknown hands had left the corn. They couldn't be from next door, since no corn grew in Mrs. Dowdel's garden.

CHAPTER TWO

Revival Dust

I tried to make August last because September, and school, didn't look good. We were not only newcomers, but we were P.K.s—preacher's kids. So everybody'd be gunning for us, and we'd be living in a fishbowl.

But not yet, not in August. Cut us this much slack. Let's get settled here in this new house before we have to take on the town. The house was okay. I had my own room.

"Let's give thanks we have an indoor bathroom," Dad said. The town was still crawling with privies and pumps, though our house and the house next door were about the only ones without television antennas. Around here you needed an antenna twice as high as your house, if you had television.

Mother stood over Ruth Ann at our side window,

gazing out past the peeling house next door to open, empty country.

"I take back every bad thing I ever thought about Terre Haute," Mother often said in a far-off voice.

We saw a lot of Mrs. Dowdel next door. There was a lot of her to see. But she never seemed to see us back. She didn't have time. On a circle of burned grass in her yard an iron pot hung from a tripod. She seemed to be pulping down apples for apple butter over a white-hot fire. She stirred an ancient paddle with holes in it. Once in a while she'd stand back to mop up under the mule hat. Then back to stirring she'd go, two-fisted on the long paddle.

"I betcha that's witch's brew in that cauldron," Ruth Ann said, very interested. "I betcha Mrs. Dowdel has warts where you can't see."

"There are no witches," Mother said. "There are only old ladies who prize their privacy."

Mrs. Dowdel weeded like a wild woman. Only when somebody passed on the road would she stand up and glance that way, running a hand down her back. Never waving. There was a bunch of boys in town, big ugly ones. They'd tramp past, heading for the crick every afternoon, punching each other. Mrs. Dowdel always watched them out of sight. She seemed to take an interest in them, but not a friendly interest. Then she'd have several sharp things to say to her tomatoes.

One evening we were just settling around the supper table. There were some slices of ham from somewhere. Mother had pulled together a potato salad out of three potatoes. We'd just joined hands. Dad began, "For what we are about to receive—"

When an almighty explosion rocked the room. Our kitchen clock stopped, and the box of matches jumped off the stove. Every nesting bird in the county took flight.

Russians, we thought, and without a Civil Defense bomb shelter for miles. Another explosion erupted and bounced off every house from here to the grain elevator.

Ruth Ann slid off her chair and was at the kitchen door. We all followed. Now Mrs. Dowdel, gray in the gloaming, loomed out from around her cobhouse. In one of her hands hung a double-barreled shotgun, an old-time Winchester 21, from the look of it. Both barrels smoked.

In her other fist she carried a pair of headless rats. They hung by their tails, and they were good-sized, almost cat-sized.

She lumbered up to her cauldron and swung the rats onto the white embers beneath. As a family, we turned away just as they burst into flame.

"This is why the Methodist Conference stuck us in this house, this so-called parsonage," Phyllis said. "Who else would live next door to her? I hate this town. I can't tell you how much."

* * *

Headless rats darted across my dreams through those nights. By day I helped Dad down at the church. There'd been a church building to spare when the two bunches of United Brethren united again. They naturally went with the better church building, brick. We got the other one. And it looked more like a corncrib than anything else—one puff of wind from a pile of kindling. Somebody'd shot out all the windows, and the roof was a sieve.

Dad had already killed a hog snake coiled in the choir loft. He and the snake met up by chance, and all Dad could think of to do was drop a box of hymnals on its head.

And if you don't like spiders, this wasn't your kind of place.

We kept busy. I sanded and shellacked the pews. Dad fitted the windows with plastic sheeting. There wasn't money for plate glass. There wasn't money for anything. We were eating off our own front porch.

Dad sang hymns while we worked: "Stand up! Stand up for Jesus." Peppy hymns. He had a fine baritone voice, only a little wobbly on the high notes. I'd jump in with some harmony for him, though I was still pretty much a soprano. "We must not! We must not! We must not suffer loss!" we sang, ringing a rafter or two. I didn't think we were half bad. But Dad was a worried man. He could do about anything with his hands. He had big hands. But it was going to take more than hammer and nails.

Over in Terre Haute he'd been assistant pastor at Third Methodist. This was the first pulpit all his own. It was going to be make-it-or-break-it for Dad here. And we hadn't seen many of those Methodists we'd heard were waiting for The Word and a preacher to bring it.

Still, we had time to get the place squared away. August was the big tent-show revival month. You couldn't get a church off the ground until the revival dust settled.

A sign appeared out by Mrs. Dowdel's mailbox:

SPARE ROOMS FOR BELIEVERS

A tent the size of Ringling Brothers' big top rose in the park uptown, the bald ground between the business block and the Norfolk & Western tracks. A giant banner stretched high between the tent poles, reading:

YOU THINK IT'S HOT <u>HERE!</u>

The number one evangelist of the sawdust circuit was coming for a week of preaching. He was Delmer "Gypsy" Piggott, well-known in his time, though his time was running out. They called him the Texas Tornado for his preaching style. He'd built a big tabernacle at Del Rio.

We didn't go that Monday night. Local preachers and their families didn't. It wasn't our kind of worship.

Besides, money in the revival's collection plate was money that never made it to ours. In a week Gypsy Piggott could scare a lot of money out of a town.

But the revival came to us. Cars and trucks parked past

our house and out of town. You could hear everything from here, four blocks from the tent. Mother tied on a fresh apron, and we sat out on our front porch, hearing the gospel quartette, four high sopranos in some very close harmony, backed up by a blare of trumpets. And they could belt out a hymn:

Don't give me no newfangled religion,
Slick as a Cadillac's fin;
Just give me that old-time religion
And the way things was back then.

Mother sighed from the porch swing.

Then Gypsy Piggott climbed onto his pulpit. They had a dynamite speaker system. The whole county could stay home and hear every word. His fist on the Bible was like an earth tremor. That collection plate rang like an alarm bell.

He didn't mince words either. He had us sinners in the fiery pit before you knew where you were. We were all on the wrong path, and Gypsy Piggott knew where it led. Liquor and bad women were mentioned. His language was pretty rough, and he had no grammar to speak of.

Mother sent Ruth Ann into the house, for all the good that would do. "It's what people want around here," Phyllis said. "That's what they're like. Why are we even here?

Nobody'll want a *real* church. I hate this podunk town."

Late that night I was jolted awake. It had to be midnight when Mrs. Dowdel's screen door banged two or three times. Feet scuffled on her back porch.

My window looked down on her place. Moonlight was slick on her tar-paper roof. Yellow light fell from the kitchen windows across her porch floor.

Stuff began to fly off the porch and bounce in her yard. Suitcases? Trumpet cases? More came. White moths seemed to flutter across the grass, but it might have been sheet music.

I couldn't see how many people were on the porch. But it was Mrs. Dowdel who barged through them and outside. She wore a nightgown the size of the revival tent. Cold moonlight hit her white hair loose in the night breeze. She held something high and poured from it onto the ground.

"'WINE IS A MOCKER, STRONG DRINK IS RAGING,'" she bellowed into the night. "Proverbs. 20:1. You could look it up. I don't have hard liquor in my house. It goes, and so do you."

She seemed to pour strong drink out on the grass. Now she hauled off and threw the bottle. She had an arm on her. The bottle glinted in moonlight, hit her cobhouse roof, and rolled off.

"Now, now, Mrs. Dowdel," a voice said, "calm yourself. 'A man hath no better thing under the sun, than to eat, and to drink, and to be merry.' Ecclesiastes. 8:15."

I'd have known that voice in the fiery pit. It was the Texas Tornado, Delmer "Gypsy" Piggott. Now I could hear Mother and Dad stirring around in their room.

My nose was flat to screen wire. "GET OFF MY PLACE," Mrs. Dowdel bellowed, "and take these . . . sopranos with you. Trumpets, strumpets—everybody out."

More shoe-scuffling came from the porch, and the peck of high heels. A sob and some squealing. The gospel quartette milled.

"You've rented your last rooms in this town, you two-faced old goat," Mrs. Dowdel thundered. The whole town was wide-awake now. "Hit the road."

"Dad-burn it, Mrs. Dowdel," the Texas Tornado whined, "we done paid you out for the whole week with ready money. Cash on the barrelhead."

"I'm about a squat jump away from a loaded Winchester 21," Mrs. Dowdel replied, "and I'm tetchy as a bull in fly time."

She turned back against a tide of sopranos and stalked into her house. Whether she was going for her gun or to bed nobody could know. The figures milled some more. A suitcase came open. But then they started for the road. A big Lincoln Continental was parked out there, washed by moonbeams. Doors banged, and the Lincoln gunned away, shaking off the dust of this town.

A room away, Mother sighed.

Then silence fell upon the listening town, and the moon slid behind a cloud. Somewhere farther out in the fields a swooping owl pounced on squealing mice. But they were faint squeaks, and far-off.

CHAPTER THREE

The Boy Next Door

Dad and I had to keep wringing out our shirts all that next day. It was a hundred in the shade, hotter inside the church. He sent me home early.

As I came past the park, they were already taking down the big revival tent—folding the tent and stealing away. They'd only managed to pass the collection plate that first night, thanks to Mrs. Dowdel. Now the Texas Tornado was having to touch down somewhere else.

People may have hated to miss the rest of revival week. But telling each other how Gypsy Piggott was chased off was interesting and some consolation. I never knew anyplace where news traveled faster. It wasn't as slow a town as it looked.

The sidewalk along the main street petered out before it came to our house. I walked out in the road with the hot concrete eating through my sneaker soles. I expect my mind wandered. It did that a lot. I remember starting to reach down and pick up a Fuller Brush on the side of the road.

Right about then I knew I wasn't alone. They came up behind me before I could think. Somebody walked up my sneaker heels. A big bruiser was suddenly on each side of me, and more of them behind.

It was the gang of big uglies who headed out this way every afternoon. Fear trickled down my spine.

A big thorny hand slipped under each one of my armpits.

"Just keep right on a-walkin'," a weirdly soft voice said far above my head. But now my feet barely grazed ground. "Just step right along, preacher's kid."

We were passing our house now, and where was my m—

"You smell funny, preacher's kid," said another voice from on high. And he should talk. "What's that you smell like?"

"Shellac," I said in a puny voice. "I been shellacking a pew."

"Pew. You can say that again," said another voice, and they all did a lot of hee-haw laughing. We must have sounded like quite a friendly bunch. But who was there to hear? We were only a ditch away from Mrs. Dowdel's yard. Was this the first time all August she hadn't been out, working her garden?

"You need to clean up and cool off, preacher's kid," came a voice. "You stink, and you're sweatin', bad. You ever been to the crick?"

I said nothing till a hand slapped the back of my head. "No."

It was open country now. We were off the slab and tramping the shimmering oiled road. Not a car on it. Not a farmer in a field. I hung between two huge hulks as the town fell away behind us. They both wore yellow steel-toed construction boots. I was just a dropkick away from being booted over the next woven-wire fence. Some big bird wheeled over us. A buzzard? A vulture?

We tramped a mile, easy. Then we were over the ditch, deep in milkwort and goldenrod. You could smell the crick before we got to the cattails and the trees. I smell it yet, slow water and pond scum and rotten logs. The smell of August, 1958.

Willows wept into the water, and I wanted to. The skeleton of an old snub-nosed rowboat was half buried in the bank. They turned me loose, and I chanced a look up at their main man. He was six foot tall. His sideburns were down to his jaw. And there was something wrong with his eyes. Now I was scared.

"Skin off them clothes," he said. "Every stitch." Now I was really scared.

But they were all skinning off their clothes. Work shirts,

jeans, a carpenter's apron, boots. Tree limbs filled up with blue denim and army surplus.

Then a giant hee-haw went up. "Underwear? Preacher's kid wears underwear? Whoooeey. Got lace on it? Git it off."

They sure weren't wearing any underwear. I had to notice, because they were so tall I only came up to their—

"Can you swim, preacher's kid?" said the tall galoot with the scary eyes.

What was the right answer? Yes? No?

"A little."

That's when I noticed they'd brought fishing line. Ten-pound fishing line, coiled in the weeds. But where were the poles? Where was the bucket of bait?

The next thing I knew I was in brown water. My nose up, then under, then up, sucking air hard. I was doing my best in that whirlpooly bend in the crick where I was just out of my depth. I was kicking hard, but that's about all I could manage with both hands tied tight behind me with fishing line. I could have used web feet. They'd thrown me pretty far out too.

But you'd be surprised how much swimming you can do with your hands tied behind you. Swimming and drowning. Four or five of the better-natured ones cheered me on from the bank. But I was going in circles, getting lower in the water.

Then with big splashes they were all in the crick, and they weren't out of their depth. They were neck and shoulders above the greasy water, batting me back and forth from one of them to the other. Back and forth.

We came back to town across country, quicker than the road. The fields were stubbly, but they let me keep my Keds. They even put them on for me and laced them up because I was still tied tight. The sneakers were all I kept. My shirt and jeans were missing, and of course the underpants had to go.

The rest of them were dressed, and cool as cucumbers after their dip in the crick. But what could I say? Nothing actually, because they'd also brought a roll of duct tape. A big patch of it was plastered over my mouth.

The trees and roofs of town rose ahead of us. I remember our long shadows rippling across the furrowed fields. Six or eight overgrown galoots and me like a piglet on a spit, hanging from two of their big, thorny mitts. They swung me over fences, and I barely cleared barbed wire. And I mean barely. The closer to town, the nakeder I felt.

They still might kill me. Though they'd gone to the trouble of hoisting me by my heels on the crick bank and shaking a gallon of brown water out of me. But they could be saving me for later.

The sun hung in the sky behind us. The day went on forever.

The nearer to town, the quieter the gang got. They

weren't that chatty anyway. In fact they only seemed to know a couple verbs. We were coming through orchards and now a melon patch. Through a stand of hollyhocks I saw the back of the last house in town, Mrs. Dowdel's. Then ours next door and our car parked around back. I was that close to home and this close to crying. But it's almost impossible to cry with your mouth taped shut. And you sure don't want your nose stopping up.

We were behind Mrs. Dowdel's property. The Japanese lantern vine growing over her privy rattled quietly. We were quieter.

"Preacher's kid," the biggest galoot sighed down in my ear, "what you've just had is a welcome to the community. It's our way of sayin' howdy. Now we're goin' to leave you in the hands of one of our solid citizens. But she ain't as friendly as us. She don't like nobody."

What?

What did this mean?

What was going to happen to me now?

Most of the gang melted away. Two of them swung me into Mrs. Dowdel's privy.

Then they went to work. I'll say this for them: They were artists with fishing line. They strung a giant spider's web that ran from rafters to loose floorboards. Then they tied me in the center, bound hand and foot and still gagged. I hung like a ham in a smokehouse just over the hole in the well-worn seat.

"Keep us in your prayers, preacher's kid," said the big one, eerie and soft.

Then they were gone. I was alone. This was about as alone as I'd ever been. Time passed, lots of it. Dimming light fell through the chinks of the privy and the half-moon carved in the door. The smell in here was truly bad. I swayed slightly in my web and tried to take a positive view of the situation. I couldn't. For one thing, my knees were higher than my ears.

It must be midnight, though daylight still came through the cracks. Maybe it was the next day? I sure would have liked to scratch my nose. But here was one good thing: They'd hung me right over the privy hole.

My mind wandered as it often did. I may have nodded off. My feet were sound asleep. Then the privy door banged open.

Filling the doorway and then some was Mrs. Dowdel. A copy of the *Farm Journal* and three corncobs were in one of her fists. I hadn't seen her up close. I'd never wanted to be anywhere near this close to her. Her specs crept to the end of her nose. We were nose to nose.

She didn't welcome surprises, and I came as one. All she'd wanted to do was use her privy, and here I was barring her way, naked as a jaybird in my own personal web.

Her old pink-rimmed eyes grew larger than her specs. She poked them back up the bridge of her nose and worked some of her chins with her free hand. I swayed. She looked my web over, up to the rafters, down to the floor. She may have admired the knots.

"Well I'll be a ring-tailed monkey if that don't about take the cake," she remarked. "And I thought I'd seen everything." I made a small sound.

She dumped her corncobs and the *Farm Journal,* and ripped the duct tape off my mouth.

"Yeoww!" I hollered.

"Had to be done," she said. "Who did you say you was?"

I coughed up something—maybe a tadpole. "I'm Bob Barnhart. The boy next door."

"Well, I can see you ain't the girl," said Mrs. Dowdel.

Over in her cobhouse hung a pair of shears for trimming the snowball bushes. Mrs. Dowdel had them in both hands now, whacking at fishing line just over my head. Sharp blades flashed. Three more whacks, and I dropped onto the worn-smooth privy seat, over the hole. She bent my head forward and reached down my back to cut my wrists loose. I couldn't feel the ends of my fingers till the next Wednesday. She hunkered down with a grunt and cut my ankles free.

"Hoo-boy," she said, "I don't truss up my Christmas turkey that tight." She wound the fishing line into a ball, since she seemed to save everything. Now without my fishing line I was nakeder than before.

"Keep your seat," she said, and went back to her cobhouse.

There was a world of tools and implements in there. A bunch of rusty rabbit traps hung on the outside wall. She rummaged around and came back with an old tarp, stiff with dried paint. She dropped it over me to cover me up. I edged off the seat, stood up, and fell in a heap of tarp on the privy floor. The blood wasn't getting to my feet yet.

"Stir them stumps and try your trotters." Mrs. Dowdel started up her back walk. "Trail me up to the house."

So I wobbled behind her up her back walk. In the tarp I must have looked like a pup tent in sneakers. It gapped in the back. I could feel breeze all the way down.

Sunlight still flooded her kitchen. The wall clock read a quarter to five. I hadn't been in the privy as long as it seemed. A big black Monarch iron range hulked along one wall. She'd never taken down a calendar. One of them read:

EVERY GOOD WISH FOR
BRIGHTER DAYS IN 1933

Mrs. Dowdel was bigger with walls around her and a ceiling. Her apron was full of bulging pockets.

She was a walking Woolworth's: a narrow-nosed handsaw, a claw hammer, clothespins, and now a ball of fishing line.

"Trail me upstairs," she mentioned. "Don't trip on your tarp."

She pulled herself up a long, shadowy flight of linoleum

stairs. I followed. She wore giant felt shoes with one button straining over the foot.

At the top of the stairs she elbowed a door open. In there dusty west light filtered through darned curtains. The windowsill was a wasp graveyard. An ancient brass bed angled out of a corner. The mattress looked like it was stuffed with cornhusks. A darker triangle showed on the wallpaper where a pennant had hung.

Mrs. Dowdel turned to a big chest and found what she was looking for: a shirt for a bigger boy than I was. It was kind of old-timey, but I hadn't come here to argue. It was faded out, but then so were my own four shirts. Three now. Out of the drawer she drew a pair of old dungarees.

"These is about the smallest I've got." She turned away to the window.

I dropped my tarp. "As to underwear," she said over her shoulder, "the only pair that comes to mind was Dowdel's, my late husband. And they'd be a hundred percent wool with buttons before and a trapdoor behind."

"No, thank you," I said, "ma'am."

The shirt had been striped at one time, but it smelled starchy and clean. I could turn up the dungaree legs, but the waist was on the wide side.

Mrs. Dowdel turned my way. The gold light pouring around her shadowed her face. But I saw right there she was somebody else. Her old hand stole up to her mouth.

She turned aside, and there was glitter behind her glasses. "Last boy wore them togs," she said, "was my grandson, Joey. That's been pretty nearly twenty-five years back. He's all growed. Don't ask me why I kept his stuff, except I keep everything. You never know."

She blinked and saw I was holding up the pants. "Lemme see what we've got for a belt." She inventoried her apron and came up with the ball of fishing line. Unwinding a shorter length, she handed it over, and I tied it around me.

"You better skin home," she said. "They may not have missed you yet. You can grow into them clothes. Do you for school."

I turned to go, ready to thank her.

"Hold it," she said, and I froze. "Who done it?"

I teetered on the doorsill in this other boy's clothes. "If I tell, I expect they'll kill me."

Mrs. Dowdel shrugged. "They may kill you anyhow."

So I admitted it was the bunch that headed out to the crick every afternoon. "Their leader's older than a kid."

"One blue eye and one green eye?" Mrs. Dowdel inquired. That was it. That's what was funny and scary about his eyes.

"That'd be Roscoe Burdick. He's Mildred's boy, and bound to be right at twenty years old. I don't know what he's still doing around these parts. At his age, most Burdicks is on the chain gang."

She gazed away, recalling everybody's family history. No secrets around here.

"As for the rest of the bunch," she said, "they're all Cowgills—Ernie's boys—and Flukes—Augie's boys—and Leapers—Elmo's boys. All dumber than stumps. Them families never was worth a toot. Not all varmints is four-legged. That bunch is the same ones who shot out all the windows in your church building."

"Do they go to school?" Suddenly I was looking ahead, into the terrible future.

"Now and again, some of them," Mrs. Dowdel said. "Not Roscoe naturally. They's teachers younger than him. He spent so many years in first grade, they named the desk for him."

Now I was looking ahead to going home, and my eyes were stinging. Last year, back in Terre Haute, when I was still a kid, I'd have gone home bawling. Now I didn't want to. And I never wanted anybody to know how Mrs. Dowdel found me in her privy. Ever.

She seemed to read my mind, or something. "I expect you can get by in that outfit till you're up in your room and into your own togs. I wouldn't worry your folks if I was you. The way I hear it, they have troubles of their own. Anyhow, they'd just tell you to turn the other cheek, wouldn't they?"

That's exactly what they'd tell me. It had to do with loving your enemies.

"Trouble is," Mrs. Dowdel observed, "after you've turned the other cheek four times, you run out of cheeks."

I couldn't figure out how to thank her. She was pointing

me out of her grandson's room. Joey's. "I've got me a spare jar of apple butter," she said. "And I baked today. You can take a loaf to your maw. Tell her you found it on the porch."

She was wheezing down the stairs behind me. The house shook. If she fell on me I was a goner. "And don't look for anything out of the law around here," she said. "The Cowgills and the Leapers is kin to the sheriff. No justice in these parts. It's every man for hisself."

I felt the town tighten around my throat.

"But as the saying goes, if you can't get justice," Mrs. Dowdel remarked, "get even."

She kept right after me all the way down to the one-hinged kitchen door. Outside, the garden and the cannas were still as an oil painting. The sinking sun was fire-red in all our side windows. Tools clanked in Mrs. Dowdel's apron pockets.

In my puniest voice I said, "You won't say anything about how you found—"

"Never set eyes on you in my life," she said, locking the screen door behind me.

CHAPTER FOUR

The Figure at the Window

Not a leaf stirred that last week of August as the world waited for school to start. The night before it did, Phyllis barged in my room without knocking.

"Stop moping in your room," she said, though she'd been moping in hers. "Let's get out of here and go for a walk or something."

Phyllis inviting me to do something? "Where?"

"I don't know," she said. "We can walk down to the school, see how long it takes."

How long could it take? You could see open country at either end of the main street.

"It's easy being you," she said. "You're just going into another grade of grade school. Nothing to it. I'm having to start high school—here. High school. Do you have the faintest idea of what that means?"

Not too much. But it sounded better than grade school to me. I thought life started when you got to high school. Grade school was just one day after another.

"If we're going for a walk, we'll have to take Ruth Ann," I said.

Phyllis slumped. This was another reminder that I had my own room while she had to share with Ruth Ann.

"I hope I come back as a boy," Phyllis said.

"From the walk?" I said.

"No, in my next life, you nincompoop."

I followed her across the hall and jumped back at her door. To help her settle in, Mother had let Phyllis paint her room in her choice of color. She'd picked a Day-Glo pink that really yelled at you. It was like being inside a stomach.

Then Phyllis had painted a stripe of that same Day-Glo pink down the center of the floor and warned Ruth Ann never to set a sandal across it.

Phyllis had hung her Elvis Presley posters, all eight of them, around both sides of the room. I know for a fact Phyllis wrote letters to Elvis Presley regularly, though she never heard back. Ruth Ann sat bunched up on her bed, clutching her dolly. Looming above her was a giant poster of Elvis in a cowboy rig and neckerchief, strumming a guitar. Another was Elvis in the gold coat he wore on his tour last year. Elvis was all swooping hair and sideburns and showing teeth in life-size sneers, all over the room. He was everywhere. It was like being in a revolving door with him.

"I'm scared," Ruth Ann said over her knees. She made big eyes up at a poster. "Don't go out and leave me with him." She whispered for fear Elvis would hear.

"We're taking you," Phyllis said. "But don't wander off from us or else. You know how you are."

Ruth Ann scooted off her bed, dragging her dolly. She'd loved it almost completely bald. Its eyes used to close. Now one was permanently closed. My eyes were still pinwheeling from the pink walls, but I saw Phyllis had laid out her first-day school outfit for tomorrow. Pencil-slim skirt and new blouse with circle pin, fresh-looking bobby socks and nearly new saddle shoes from the Goodwill store in Terre Haute. We made a lot of sacrifices for Phyllis.

To copy her, Ruth Ann had laid out her dress too, the shiny plaid one that did her for church. Matching ribbons for her braids. She had about a month's wear left in her sandals.

Girls take their time, but we were finally ready. Phyllis wore her sundress with the jacket in case we met anybody on the street. She'd scrubbed her sneakers. I have to admit she was a real pretty girl, though whether that would do her any good at this school, who knew?

"Stay on the lighted street," Mother called after us.

Out on the porch Ruth Ann plunked her dolly into

the doll buggy. She never traveled light. We were lucky she didn't bring her hula hoop. She bumped the buggy down the steps.

"Why are you taking that thing?" Phyllis wanted to know.

"She hasn't been out all day," Ruth Ann said. "She needs some air. She's practically gasping." She meant her doll, named Grachel. Don't even ask why. For a name I think she couldn't decide between Grace and Rachel, and she only had one doll.

"And what's this about?" Phyllis reached into the buggy and pulled up a quart jar with holes punched in the lid.

"For lightning bugs in case we need to see our way home," Ruth Ann said. She always had a plan.

When we got to where the sidewalk started, it was evening under the trees. We came past the church. A lot of the plastic sheeting over the windows had blown out.

Farther along, the lights of uptown flickered, and the red light on top of the grain elevator across the tracks. The evening St. Louis to Chicago train roared through with its Vista Dome cars all lit up. People having dinner in the dining car blurred past. The town trembled.

There was a hole in the business block where the cafe used to be. Now it was a Dairy Queen frozen custard stand, buzzing with fluorescent lights. Not that we had any loose change for a frozen custard. But it was the only place in town to be.

Cars and Harleys were pulled up. Even a tractor. Kids hung around. Big kids. A lot of denim and boots.

"Keep walking," Phyllis said out of the side of her mouth.

Girls and guys lounged around in their separate groups. The guys were all buzz cuts and ducktails. Everybody was a ghastly color from the fluorescent light, like from another planet. Gum stopped snapping when we came on the scene.

From a car radio Elvis Presley's voice wavered out:

"If you cain't come around, at least, please, uh, telyphone."

Phyllis quivered slightly at the sound of Elvis's voice. But she pulled herself together. "Stroll," she mouthed. "Don't hurry."

I wanted to break into a run. The crowd parted for us a little. A very little. A brassy girl with kind of rowdy red hair leaned right over Ruth Ann's doll buggy for a better look at Phyllis. I was working hard not to meet anybody's stare.

The cars pulled up were mostly pre-war Plymouths and a couple of muddy trucks. Sprawled across the hood of an old DeSoto was a big galoot propped up on his elbows. I was looking right at him, and I'd know that face anywhere. Those eyes. One blue. One green.

Roscoe Burdick. A cigarette wedged over his ear, and a cigarette pack was folded up into his T-shirt sleeve. Lucky

Strikes. But he didn't even see me. He only had eyes for Phyllis. He worked his chin from sideburn to sideburn with one of his big thorny hands and gave her a deep blue-and-green stare. It was like he'd never seen a girl before. The other girls were looking her over too, up and down, up and down. It took us about a year and a half to stroll past the whole bunch.

When we were finally down by the Stubbs & Askew insurance agency, a long low wolf whistle came out of the crowd behind us. Then a lot of hee-haw laughing. Then Elvis again, moaning out of a tinny car radio, "Don't be cruel to a heart that's . . ."

We moved on into the night to the last slab of sidewalk. The town ran out, and there was the school out in a field. It was a new yellow brick, since the war. A consolidated school with a lot of blacktop for the buses. The rope pinged on the flagpole. You could feel the whole place hunkered down in the dark, just waiting for tomorrow.

"What's that, Bobby?" Ruth Ann pulled up her buggy.

"That's it," I told her. "School. We'll all three be in the same building." I figured she'd like that.

"Us?" she said in a wispy voice. "When?"

Phyllis sighed one of Mother's sighs. Even I saw the problem. All along Ruth Ann had been thinking that after summer was over, we'd go back to Terre Haute, and everything would be the way it used to be. She'd only laid out her school clothes because Phyllis did. She was barely six and sort of lived in her own world. Sometimes we forgot to spell things out for her. It was dark, but you knew she was getting teary.

"It'll be all right," Phyllis told her. "You'll be in first grade, and everybody will be new. And you know your numbers and your letters. It'll be fine. Little kids aren't as mean as big kids."

I wasn't so sure about that. But I gave Phyllis credit for saying so.

Ruth Ann gripped her buggy handle. Her knuckles were white in the dark. "Then we're staying here?" Her voice wobbled.

Phyllis and I both sighed.

"But how will he find me?" Ruth Ann said.

"Who?" we said.

"You know who," Ruth Ann said. "You know perfectly well."

I didn't. But Phyllis rolled her eyes, then caught mine. Over Ruth Ann's head she quietly spelled out a couple of words, a name.

"S-A-N-T-A," Phyllis spelled, "C-L-A-U-S."

We weren't about to walk home past the Dairy Queen again. We picked a darker street. People didn't sit out on their porches much anymore. A blue television glow came out of nearly every house and frosted the yard.

Even in Terre Haute we hadn't had a television set.

Some people thought it wasn't the kind of thing a preacher's family should have. It didn't set a good example. Anyway, Mother said it was bad for our eyes.

So on nights this dark back in Terre Haute we'd scouted around the neighborhood till we found a television in plain sight through a front window. We'd stand in their bushes and watch it.

Now we were at it again.

We came to a blue-lit window. The curtains were open, but the shrubs were low and sparse, so we'd be in the open. Still, we veered off the sidewalk and drifted up to the house. Phyllis and I made a cradle seat with our hands, and Ruth Ann climbed aboard.

We hoisted her up, and now we were these three heads at the window. But it was okay. The people in there were facing away to the screen, eating popcorn. You could smell melted butter. They were watching an advertisement for a car. A commercial. Words appeared on the screen.

"What do they say?" Ruth Ann whispered.

"There's a Ford in your future," I read. "Make sure it's an Edsel."

The screen jumped to wrestling. Ruth Ann bounced. She loved wrestling. Phyllis didn't. She was always wanting it to be Sunday night and Elvis making a surprise appearance on the *Ed Sullivan Show*.

But wrestling was good because you didn't need to

hear anything. The wrestlers boomeranged off the ropes and into each other. They were big bruisers. The biggest, blondest, baddest was named Gorgeous George, a major star.

"Kill him, Gorgeous," Ruth Ann whispered. "Twist off his ears." There was a whistle in her whisper because she was missing her two front teeth. "Take him apart, limb from limb," she whispered, making little fists.

"Come on, let's go," Phyllis murmured. "I can't hold her any longer. I'm numb."

Ruth Ann dropped into a shrub, and we stole away.

Now we were running out of sidewalk and only a turning from home. Ruth Ann jumped for lightning bugs, but they were all out of reach. It was getting late, and it was a school night.

But then we came to a house with a good strong blue glow through thick evergreens. It was too good to pass up, and dark as pitch under the trees of the yard. We crept forth, close, like some six-legged creature of the night. You couldn't see where your feet went.

I tripped over something, like a leaf bag but bigger. I made some sound.

"Shut up," Phyllis whispered. What had I fallen over? It felt like a gunny sack stuffed tight with something. I reached around inside.

"What is it?" Phyllis whispered.

"Ears of corn," I said.

We edged around it. Ruth Ann clung to us. The glow from a big screen beamed through the branches. We edged up till pine needles poked our faces. It began to smell like Christmas.

We were only one branch from the house when we saw it. The shape. A figure stood in the shrubs, looking in the window. There before us and way bigger. Darker than the night.

My blood ran cold. Phyllis's hands clamped her mouth and Ruth Ann's. We froze. I was scared speechless. The shrubbery was a cage now, and the branches were claws. The massive back of the black figure was as near us as I am to you and big as a bear. Its huge, thick arms came up, turning and twisting against the blue light. Ruth Ann clung. The figure bobbed and weaved, mirroring Gorgeous George on the television inside as he worked over his helpless victims. At least it's a sports fan, I thought.

A hand closed over my arm. I flinched. It was Phyllis. She seemed to jerk her head. We needed to edge back very light on our feet. The big figure before us was still grabbing for night air, still ducking, helping Gorgeous George tie his enemies in knots.

Step by step we eased out of the bushes, skirting the corn sack. Ruth Ann was as silent as the ghost of a girl. We walked backward to the first tree and the doll buggy. Then we lit out. When our porch light was in sight, Phyllis drew up, fighting for breath.

"I'm scared," Ruth Ann whimpered. "What did you bring me for?"

"You know who that was, don't you?" Phyllis said. "That . . . figure at the window. It was Mrs. Dowdel."

I guessed it made sense. Like us, she didn't have her own television. Or any sweet corn in her garden. Looked like she'd been harvesting it by night out of somebody else's. Then she'd stopped to go a round or two along with Gorgeous George. Phyllis moaned.

"This town," she said, hopeless, "this town . . ."

A car went past, slow. It was one-eyed. I'd have thought it must be an old DeSoto with a slipping clutch and a Hollywood muffler. It gunned into open country, and the dark swallowed its taillights.

Personally I thought it was time to call it a night. Ruth Ann began to unpack her buggy. She stopped. I can still see her hands hovering over the doll blanket in the porch light.

"Grachel's gone," she said in her smallest voice. It was a bad moment.

"Feel around in there for her," Phyllis said.

"She's gone," Ruth Ann said.

"Maybe she fell out," I said. "Maybe—"

"She was wedged in under the bug jar," Phyllis murmured.

"She didn't fall out," Ruth Ann said. "I know where she went."

"Where?"

"Back to Terre Haute where he can find her. She went home. I wish I could."

We never saw the doll buggy again. I guess Ruth Ann put it in the pile to go to Goodwill, where it came from to begin with. I guess she didn't want it around.

CHAPTER FIVE

The Afternoon of the Turtle

I walked Ruth Ann home after the first day of school. She looked a little pale, a little droopy. But she'd hung on to her Davy Crockett lunch bucket. Which was better than what happened to me. Two big bozos who were repeating sixth grade stole my lunch.

They were Newt Fluke and Elmo Leaper, Jr. Both about five ten, and Newt shaved. They also happened to be a couple of the big uglies who'd thrown me into Salt Crick. Anyway, I'd saved back an apple in my desk, the way you do when you're not one of the bigger kids.

Ruth Ann took my hand across the street, and I let her. Nobody was looking.

"How'd you like first grade?" I asked because she wasn't saying.

"It was all right. We cut out fall leaves from construction paper," she said. "But I thought by afternoon we'd be reading. What are nits?"

Nits? "Ah," I said. "Well, they're louse eggs or baby louses. Lice. Something like that. Why?"

"The teacher checked in our hair for them."

Oh. "Did she find any?"

"She found a lot on a girl named Ida-Belle Eubanks. My desk has a name."

"Roscoe?"

Ruth Ann nodded.

Mrs. Dowdel had fired up her cauldron that afternoon. I noticed from my window when I was upstairs messing around in my room. She was boiling shucked sweet corn in batches. She pitchforked the ears in and out. Smoke billowed up around her.

I looked again, and there was Ruth Ann on the far side of the cannas. Mother had captured her long enough to get her out of her school dress and into coveralls. Now Ruth Ann was over by the hollyhocks, already deep into Mrs. Dowdel's territory.

She'd pulled off a few blossoms to make up a little family of hollyhock dolls. Without Grachel, Ruth Ann was kind of lost and alone in the world. She used hollyhock buds for heads and upside-down flowers for the skirts. That kind of business. Toothpicks for arms.

Ruth Ann was helping herself to the hollyhocks, and Mrs. Dowdel was pitchforking her bubbling corn. The distance was narrowing between them. But each one was in a separate world—busy.

Then pretty soon Mrs. Dowdel dropped her pitchfork and headed off to her cobhouse. She practically ran Ruth Ann down. But neither one paid any attention to the other. When Mrs. Dowdel came back, she was lugging a crate with something on top. A big mixing bowl? Who knows? She did all kinds of things in her yard most people do indoors.

She planted the bowl on the ground and tipped the crate. Something rolled out. From up here it looked like a rusty hubcap, but bigger. It was there in the grass. Then it moved, by itself. Ruth Ann watched.

It was a turtle, a great big thing. It started crawling toward the fire, thought better of that, and made a slow turtle-turn. Mrs. Dowdel stood over it, keeping an eye on it, taking her time. Ruth Ann was right there, in her shadow.

There was a stick in Mrs. Dowdel's hand, no longer than a clothespin. She bent to tease the turtle with it, and I guess he fell for it. I couldn't really see from up here, but he stuck his neck out of his shell. Bad idea. A turtle will take your finger off, especially if you bother it. Mrs. Dowdel, bent double, invited the turtle to take a bite out of the stick she was offering between two careful fingers.

Ruth Ann tucked her fingers into her armpits. She was all eyes.

The turtle must have chomped down on the stick, because Ruth Ann jumped.

Out of her apron Mrs. Dowdel drew a businesslike knife. It flashed once, and the turtle, who wouldn't stop biting the stick, couldn't pull his head back in his shell. The head flew. Ruth Ann jumped a foot. With a big shoe Mrs. Dowdel kicked the turtle head into the fire.

Now she was squatting in the yard. A turtle can crawl till sunset after it's lost its head. She flipped it over, and it lolled.

I couldn't see this part at all, but Mrs. Dowdel had gone to work running the knife around the shell to cut it loose from the skin, sawing in a circle. I could only see this happening in Ruth Ann's face. She was as interested as she'd ever been in anything in her life.

Mrs. Dowdel seemed to work the skin off the turtle's feet. She lifted the shell like the lid off a stew pot and set it rolling away toward a garden row. Ruth Ann watched it go.

Finally Mrs. Dowdel heaved herself upright. With a small mess of turtle guts in her cupped hands, she went over to the fire and threw them in. Ruth Ann's mouth hung open. She was all eyes and mouth. Even her braids looked interested.

Mrs. Dowdel worked over the rest of the turtle, carving up the parts you can eat to fry for her supper. She didn't bring over any for us, but there's not a lot of eating in one turtle.

But the point is from that day on, the afternoon of the turtle, Ruth Ann was Mrs. Dowdel's shadow. And Mrs. Dowdel let her be. Ever after, Ruth Ann seemed to forget she'd ever lived in Terre Haute, or anywhere but here.

Phyllis didn't get home till five on that particular afternoon. There'd been high school meetings about upcoming fall events: a sock hop, a hayride, corn-husking, homecoming. Somebody gave her a ride home.

Counting us Barnharts, nine people showed up at Dad's first service that next Sunday. I ushered, wearing a white shirt and a necktie of Dad's. It was longer than my fly. I could have put everybody in one pew, but I scattered them around. Still, Dad could count, and it wasn't much of a turnout.

One lady wore a Mackinaw jacket and a hat with a veil. Her eyes were all over the place, and her teeth came out to meet you.

"I ain't Methodist," she warned me as I steered her at a pew. "I'm from the church across the tracks, so I'm wash-foot. I'm just here to see how the heathens worship." She grinned quite friendly through her veil, and her teeth were a real assortment. She said she was Mrs. Wilcox.

Mother sat up front in her summer dress. Next to her

was Ruth Ann with six or eight hollyhock dolls to fill out the pew. Phyllis sat on the back row, writing a letter. I passed the plate. Pollen blew in through the torn windows. Dad said, "Let us make a joyful noise," and we tried a hymn, "Blessed Assurance." But we tapered off.

Dad cut his sermon short so we'd be out ahead of the United Brethren. The wash-foot congregation across the tracks went on for another hour. Mrs. Wilcox had time to catch it on her way home.

After church we counted out the offering on our kitchen table. A dollar twelve, and two meat ration tokens from World War II and a small scattering of S&H Green Stamps.

"Great oaks from little acorns grow," Dad said, not too certain. Mother didn't look certain at all.

Mrs. Dowdel hadn't turned up, but it was well known that she wasn't a church woman. Where would she find the time? As the fall days got shorter, hers got longer. She'd put up a carload of corn relish. The labels on the Ball jars were written out in a hand that looked like Ruth Ann's printing, though she'd had help with the spelling.

CORN RELISH
1958

It was getting harder to keep Ruth Ann home. Mother about gave up trying.

A jar of corn relish rolled all the way over onto our porch. The tarp I'd once worn was stretched on Mrs. Dowdel's side yard, thick with drying black walnuts. The stove lengths began to rise in piles on her back porch. She could see winter from here.

I couldn't, of course. I couldn't see a day ahead. Typical of me, the next time trouble broke out next door, I was sound asleep.

The Fall of the Year

CHAPTER SIX

The Haunted Melon Patch

Evidently Mrs. Dowdel always had extra trouble in the fall of the year. Nameless figures were known to sneak down behind the houses to her patch and swipe her melons. It was kind of a local tradition. Dating couples had been flushed out of this same location.

The town knew Mrs. Dowdel was armed and dangerous. But high school kids would figure that trying to steal a half-ripe watermelon was worth the risk of getting your head blown off.

Even after her long days, Mrs. Dowdel sat guard down there. You could see her on sentry duty from our back porch. She made herself pretty comfortable. There was a nip in the air now, but she'd put together a little stove from cinderblocks and an oven rack. A pot of camp coffee brewed on the grille. She buried baking potatoes under the fire. There she hunkered on two overturned pails in a cap with flaps and three or four afghans. Her melons and squash were coming on. Behind her on the vines climbing the cobhouse, her gourds were ready.

So was she. The Winchester was always across her big knees, unless she was cleaning it by firelight.

Maybe sitting out in the hazy night, watching the sparks rise to join the stars, gave Mrs. Dowdel ideas. Maybe she even saw weird visions in the firelight's flicker. Who knows?

A rumor about that particular melon patch began to drift through town. At first it wasn't louder than the whisper of dry leaves. A word here. A word there. It could have come from anywhere. Then it broke into print in the county seat newspaper. A column called "News From Our Outlying Communities" appeared in the *Piatt County Call:*

STRANGE SIGHTINGS
IN RURAL VICINITY

According to Mrs. Dowdel, a lifelong resident, there is no truth to the story making the rounds of one of our smaller villages. In a melon patch at the rear of the Dowdel property, rumor reports that an Unexplained Presence has been sighted by various intruders in the dark of night. Young couples have fled the patch in terror, leaving behind half-empty bottles of Thunderbird wine, picnic blankets, and several transistor radios.

"Horsefeathers," Mrs. Dowdel is quoted as saying, or a very similar word. "I ain't seen a thing out of the ordinary, and I'm in my patch very nearly every night to discourage the juvenile delinquents who is taking over the town."

However, the elderly landowner admitted that her property and outbuildings are built over an ancient Kickapoo burial ground.

"Oh pshaw," Mrs. Dowdel expostulated. "As kids we was forever digging up arrowheads and calabashes and all them ancient relics. Beadwork and such stuff. Once in a great while a skull would surface, or a dog would dig up something."

And the Unexplained Presence?

"Some used to say they'd seen the ghost of a girl in a feathered headdress and moccasins," Mrs. Dowdel recalled. "You know how people talk. They called her the Kickapoo Princess."

When our reporter inquired if she'd ever seen the ghostly Kickapoo Princess herself, the aged matron replied, "Me? I got enough aggravation from the living without messing with the dead."

Asked for a final word on the subject, Mrs. Dowdel said, "Keep off my property. You know who you are. The next ghost you see could be you."

After this news broke, the rumor of spooky doings in the melon patch spread far out into the county.

A steady line of cars and trucks edged along our street every evening, bumper to bumper. People craned their necks for a glimpse of anything they could see. Flashbulbs popped from backseats. Mrs. Dowdel's cobhouse blocked most of the view. But people could see the glow of her campfire like an eerie halo above.

"You children," Mother said in a weary voice, "keep completely out of this. Where's Ruth Ann?"

In a day or two the police chief and the newspaper were swamped with reports of strange lights in the night and sudden sounds.

We Barnharts were used to sudden sounds by now. It was the hunting season, at least in Mrs. Dowdel's mind. Pintails, mallards, teals, the first of the migrating Canada geese often flapped their last over her property. Any time before dark you were apt to hear the full voice of a twelve-gauge shotgun. Then something on the wing would stop short in the sky and drop like a rock. And whether it was actually pheasant season or not, it was too late to warn the pheasant.

Another week or so, and rumors of the ghost princess began to blend with last year's big news. People remembered how the Russians had sent their two Sputnik rockets into orbit, one with a dog riding in it. This brought back the topic of flying saucers.

Mrs. L. J. Weidenbach, the banker's wife, granted an interview with the *Piatt County Call.* She spoke for the membership of the Daughters of the American Revolution, saying:

"The Russians are perfectly capable of disguising one of their spies as the ghost of an Indian princess or anything else of either sex, not to mention a flying dog. The enemy is already among us. We're probably radioactive already. We must keep our eyes peeled and support our troops."

Over on the high school side, the kids were abuzz. They'd all trespassed on the haunted melon patch at one time or another. But nobody could finger the couples who'd left the Thunderbird wine and picnic blankets and transistor radios behind when the Kickapoo Princess scared them off. A few began to remember they'd seen something they couldn't put a name to in the melon patch. They milled in the school halls and couldn't settle. Test scores dropped. A Boy Scout troop working toward Eagle said there ought to be a badge for Ghost Spotting.

The whole matter might have died down, with football season and corn-husking and high school homecoming on the way. But things took another turn on a certain moonless night. And it wasn't Boy Scouts. It was girls, a bunch of them. I slept through most of it, up till the screaming and gunfire. But by daybreak the whole town had all the particulars.

Though high school sororities weren't allowed, there *was* one, run by a redhead named Waynetta Blalock. Her mother had been a Lovejoy, and they owned the hybrid seed corn and the grain elevator. The sorority was Iota Nu Beta, which some people said stood for I Oughta Know Better.

This was the time of year Iota Nu Beta initiated new freshmen girls. Not Phyllis. She said herself she wasn't eligible since she couldn't wear makeup and only had two skirts. Waynetta had said all over school that Phyllis was "poor as a church mouse and anyhow not *from* here."

Even down in the grades we heard all about the plans for a secret Iota Nu Beta initiation. Waynetta personally leaked word that it would take place in the vicinity of the Haunted Melon Patch.

On that moonless Friday night, according to eyewitnesses, the Iota Nu Beta girls met out behind our house, by our car. We had a car. We just didn't have gas money for it, and it burned a quart of oil if you hit the starter. It was a 1950 Nash four-door. We called it the Pickle because of its shape. Also it was green.

From over by the parked Pickle the sorority girls could see across the cannas. There Mrs. Dowdel slumped asleep before her dying fire. Out there on flat ground she must have looked like the Rock of Gibraltar. Her shotgun lay broken open and was beginning to slip off her knees. The scene was silent as the grave except for a little ground wind rattling the gourd vine against the cobhouse.

The first girl to be initiated—first and last—was Barbara Jean Jeeter. She wore babydoll shorty pajamas and Spooly plastic curlers. She had to crawl out in the patch, steal a squash within range of Mrs. Dowdel, and crawl back. The other part of the initiation, to eat a lard sandwich and recite a dirty limerick, was slated for later back at Waynetta's house.

Edna-Earl Stubbs and Vanette Pankey, the sorority sergeants at arms, gave Barbara Jean a kick to start her out. Even if she didn't believe in ghosts, she had to believe in Mrs. Dowdel's shotgun. So she belly-crawled low, and it would have been pretty dank down in that sandy soil for a girl dressed in as little as Barbara Jean was. But freshmen will do anything to belong.

Barbara Jean crept on, from melon to melon, from squash to squash. At this point eyewitness reports differ. Vanette Pankey said that even from the Pickle she heard a sound, a rattle of dried beans in a gourd. Edna-Earl Stubbs said no. The first sound was a distant drumbeat, very far-off. Boom, boom, boom—like that. Anyway, it didn't wake Mrs. Dowdel.

Then we come to some real confusion. Firelight played against the cobhouse wall. The gourd vine cast fluttering shadows. Waynetta herself said she was the first to see somebody or something standing there, the vines grown up around her. Some creature of the night, or history. Not quite life-size, but definitely there. Another sorority girl said no. The first sighting of the ghost was right up by Mrs. Dowdel, like it had just stepped out from behind her. Or floated. With firelight on its face.

Wrong, Edna-Earl said. She clearly saw the Kickapoo Princess descending from a great height, probably heaven or the Happy Hunting Ground. Edna-Earl saw a pair of beaded moccasins dangling a good six feet above the ground. Maybe higher.

They were all scared too speechless to warn Barbara Jean. But they all agreed on one point: The Kickapoo Princess was wearing a full feathered headdress and carried a pair of gourd rattles in her weirdly pale little hands. And they all said her hair was in braids.

Anyway, here came Barbara Jean through the melons, working along on her elbows. She was within reach of the dying fire and spotting for squash when she heard something or saw something. She jumped up before she thought, stumbled and fell back. Then sat down hard.

Everybody over by the Pickle heard a snapping sound. Barbara Jean sent up a scream that tore the night in two.

"HELP!" she shrieked. "I been grabbed. The ghost's dragging me with her into her grave. SAVE ME!"

Barbara Jean was heard uptown. She certainly brought Mrs. Dowdel around. She vaulted out of deep sleep, and her pails went over behind her. She fished two shells out of her apron and fed them into the shotgun. Shouldering the butt of the gun into her afghans, she swung wildly.

"Hold your fire!" Barbara Jean screamed. "I'm already half buried, and the ghost is biting me right on my—"

KABOOM, KABOOM. Mrs. Dowdel fired twice. A tongue of red flame from each barrel licked the night. People all over the township called the chief of police.

Barbara Jean's screams knocked me out of bed. Then the gunplay. When I came out of my room, the door to Phyllis and Ruth Ann's was closed. How could they sleep through this? I wondered. Downstairs Mother and Dad were on the back porch, wearing blankets. The Pickle stood alone. Seeing a sorority sister in dire danger, the Iota Nu Betas had all hightailed it home to save their own skins. As president, Waynetta Blalock was no doubt in the lead.

Mrs. Dowdel had already released Barbara Jean from the steel jaws of a spring-action rabbit trap, which had a good firm hold on her where it hurts most.

Now the red light on the police chief's Dodge lit up everything. There was enough light to explain any Unexplained Presence. Mrs. Dowdel stood with one hand on her hip, and the shotgun in the crook of her other arm. She'd raised one flap on her cap to hear what Police Chief C. P. Snokes had to say.

He was as well-armed as she was. But she could outdraw him. "Doggone it, Mrs. Dowdel, discharging a firearm within the city limits is a crime."

"So's trespassing." Mrs. Dowdel nodded down at Barbara

Jean still sprawled among the melons. "Anyhow, who says we're inside the city limits?"

A crowd was gathering out at the edge of the light, people from all around the neighborhood in the darnedest array of sleepwear you ever saw.

"The County Surveyor says so," C. P. Snokes said. "You know yourself the city limits is that woven-wire fence that runs along the west side of your property."

"Do tell." Mrs. Dowdel poked at her fire with a big shoe. "You talking white man's law? I'd say this ancient Kickapoo burial ground was here long before the first so-called pioneers."

C. P. Snokes scratched up under his cap. "Mrs. Dowdel, are you telling me you live on an Indian reser—"

"I reserve the right to protect my property is what I'm telling you. Run that gal in," Mrs. Dowdel said. "Read her her rights and book her like they do on the television."

C. P. Snokes's flashlight revealed a no-nonsense, heavy-duty patented rabbit trap nearby Barbara Jean. "That's a mean-lookin' rabbit trap," C. P. Snokes said.

"But legal," Mrs. Dowdel said.

"Catch many rabbits?"

"Caught one tonight," she said. "Looks like a snowshoe hare."

Sure enough, in the flashlight's beam Barbara Jean looked a lot like a scared white rabbit in plastic hair curlers and shorty pajamas. Her eyes were pink in the glare. Her nose twitched, though she was still too scared to cry.

C. P. Snokes got a good look at her. "Doggone it, I can't run her in."

"How come?" Mrs. Dowdel said.

"She's the Jeeter girl, the doctor's daughter. And her mama was a—"

"I know what her mama was," Mrs. Dowdel said. "Tell her to keep her gal home at night. My motto is, 'Ready, Fire, Aim.' Keep that in mind. Next time there won't be enough of her left to initiate."

That pretty well rounded out the night. C. P. Snokes put Barbara Jean in his Dodge. Now she was crying buckets, though he was only taking her home to the Jeeters out on the LaPlace road. The seat of her shorty pajamas hung in tatters. Barbara Jean was crying her eyes out, but she had a good grip on a medium-sized acorn squash.

Mrs. Dowdel kicked ashes on her embers and went on up to the house, the Winchester over her arm. In these last hours before dawn, the town tried to settle.

I couldn't, and was still wide-awake to hear a stealthy foot on the stairs. I peered out of my room just as Phyllis's form vanished into hers. I followed.

She nearly jumped over the bed when I turned up there on her heels. Still, she had the sense not to scream. The envelope to a letter she was writing to Elvis Presley was on her table:

Private Elvis Presley
"A" Company
First Medium Tank Battalion
32nd Regiment
Fort Hood, Texas.

She moved between me and it. But I had reason to know she signed all her letters to Elvis,

Love me tender, Phyllis

Ruth Ann slept with a night-light. The Elvises loomed over her. The Elvis over Phyllis's bed glowed in the dark. It was from the *Jailhouse Rock* movie.

"Close that door," Phyllis whispered at me. "What are you doing up at this—"

"The whole town's up," I whispered back. "Big doings in the melon patch. Haunts, gunfire, sorority girls, the law. You can't hear yourself think. We thought you went to bed early."

"I did," Phyllis said, somewhat shifty. "Then I got up and . . . went on a hayride."

"I thought the Future Farmers hayride was next week-end."

"It is," Phyllis whispered, not looking me in the eye.

There were little bits of straw and hay all over her, from her barrettes to her penny loafers. Her rolled-up jeans were dusty with chaff.

"Mother and Dad didn't know you sneaked out," I accused.

"I didn't sneak out," she said. "I left quietly. I'm fourteen. I have a life to live. In many important ways I'm practically twenty."

"Oh," I said.

"And clear out of my room," Phyllis whispered. It loomed pink around us. "Ruth Ann will wake up, and it'll be your fault."

We glanced across the pink stripe to Ruth Ann's side. She was this little mound in the bed, snoring lightly, with one small hand on top of the covers. A drying hollyhock doll nestled by her chin.

"For Pete's sake," Phyllis murmured, "what are those feathers doing all around her bed? It looks like a pheasant flew in here and blew up."

Chapter Seven

Fuss and Feathers

The town was all eyes and ears, and the countryside heard all about it. The Kickapoo Princess had gone overnight from rumor to sure thing. Being high school girls, the witnesses weren't reliable. But there was a bunch of them, and they sang like canaries.

It was a story that had everything: ghosts, gunplay, and Civil Defense.

WHAT'S GOING ON IN A RURAL PIATT COUNTY MELON PATCH?

a headline in the *Champaign Courier* inquired.

ARE OUR DISTANT EARLY WARNING DEFENSE SYSTEMS ENOUGH?

People who couldn't find us on a map beat a path to our door. Traffic backed up, and the newspapers of Arcola, Sullivan, and DeWitt County sent reporters.

Woody's Zephyr Oil filling station pumped gas around the clock. The Dairy Queen took on extra help and was talking about putting in a drive-through. A lot of money changed hands.

Barbara Jean Jeeter's mother kept her out of school for a week, saying she had a beast of a cold and possibly bronchitis.

To cash in, Mrs. Dowdel had set up shop out at the front of her property. It was a roadside stand featuring her jars of corn relish and apple butter and everything else out of her storm cellar. Piles of jars stood on hay bales, though she had no hay to bale. There were big bunches of bittersweet tied with fishing line. Shocks of Indian corn rose out of pumpkin piles. A few gawky dolls made out of cornhusks and yarn, with walnuts for faces.

A sign over a mountain of watermelon and mushmelon read:

**PRODUCE FROM THE HAUNTED PATCH
YOU PLUG 'EM YOU BOUGHT 'EM**

Coffee cans held displays of pheasant feathers:

**AUTHENTIC KICKAPOO HEADDRESS
FEATHERS 5¢ APIECE 3 FOR A DIME**

Mrs. Dowdel's prices were steep, but she was making money hand over fist. Also, she was unusually chatty to reporters who wanted to interview her, though they had to buy a gallon jug of soft cider or a peck of peaches first.

You could hear her from our house, bending the reporters' ears. "Pshaw, if you're after a story, go down to the southern part of the state, down there at Cahokia. I know it's the rough end of creation, but the old prehistoric people buried their folks in mounds down there. A good many has been dug up and put on display. Bones, of course. Go on down there and don't bother me," she'd say, and keep the change.

A small figure joined her after school, waiting on trade and darting back and forth for more gourds off the haunted vine at a dime apiece, a quarter for three. It was Ruth Ann in a cut-down version of Mrs. Dowdel's feedsack apron, with pockets.

Mother kind of gave up and said, "At least I know where she is, and she doesn't have to cross a busy street." To work on his sermons, Dad had to move up in the attic. The traffic was deafening, and cars parked in our front yard.

Ruth Ann only came home in time for supper, bobbing through the cannas in an apron that brushed her sandals. She never came home empty-handed. She'd bring a mess of tomatoes too bruised to sell. Or a long-necked squash Mother could fry in butter. Now Ruth Ann was tying up her braids at the back of her head, since most of Mrs. Dowdel's hair was drawn back in a big bun. Ruth Ann carried a corn dolly in her apron pocket now that the hollyhocks were over. If you asked me, she was turning into a Mrs. Dowdel doll herself.

Mother tried to have little talks with her. "Honey, you're a good little helper, bless your heart, but try to remember Mrs. Dowdel is old and can get confused in the things she says."

"Pshaw," Ruth Ann would say back, "this whole town is built where two old Indian trails crossed. The Kickapoos goin' one way, the Illini the other. Hoo-boy, no wonder they's restless spirits underfoot." Then she'd poke at the bridge of her nose like she wore spectacles.

Mother sighed.

Mrs. Dowdel turned a tidy profit. Her apron got so saggy with loose change that she had to hang a berry pail from an army surplus ammo belt slung around her big middle.

Another rumor began to drift through town, lazy like the smoke off the burning leaves. You could probably have traced it back to Mrs. Dowdel herself. It was common knowledge that she didn't trust banks, especially the Weidenbachs' bank uptown. Still, she was spotted at the teller's counter, picking up those papers you roll piles of quarters in. The bank gave them out free.

She was said to have folding money in stacks too—stacks and stacks. The exact amount grew in the telling. Her front room light burned late as she sat counting it, several said. Rumor reported that she was stashing her treasure somewhere in her house. A loose floorboard in her grandson's old bedroom was mentioned. Joey's room. But witnesses were on the record that she'd been digging out in her melon patch in the darkest part of night. Who knew?

Finally Mrs. Dowdel had sold every melon and squash in her patch, every gourd off her vine. And all at top dollar. Her tomato plants were picked clean and ready to be dug under. The pheasant feathers had sold like hot cakes. They'd flown out of those coffee cans.

She'd feathered her nest for sure. Now you'd think she'd be hunkering down for winter and maybe paying to have her kindling split. But no.

She turned up at our kitchen door one night. A heavy clump on the porch, a thundering rap on the door, and there she was. From the table we saw the two moons of her specs agleam in the gloom. We jumped.

Supper was just over, and Phyllis was plotting her escape. Ruth Ann went to open the door, and we followed. Then we saw she wasn't alone. An eerie face under a mashed hat peered around her. Cross-eyes peered at us and everywhere else, through a veil. It was Mrs. Wilcox of the wash-foot church.

Mrs. Dowdel leaned toward Mother and muttered, "I couldn't shake her." She jerked a thumb to indicate Mrs. Wilcox. "She's all over me like a rubber girdle in a heatwave."

"Oh, but you're both as welcome as you can be," Mother said. "Come in and take chairs."

But that wasn't going to happen. They came in, though, single-file. They were paying a call, so they had on their best aprons, with rickrack. Mrs. Wilcox's eyes and teeth went in every direction. Something bulky hung in the crook of Mrs. Dowdel's arm. Not her Winchester. It was a box, a little bigger than a shoebox.

Phyllis held back, trying not to be there. Ruth Ann and I were the only ones who'd seen Mrs. Dowdel this close, and I wasn't admitting it. But she looked straight over my head like she'd never set eyes on me in her life. Ruth Ann's apron was just like hers and Mrs. Wilcox's. Phyllis was drifting farther off.

"I don't neighbor," Mrs. Dowdel announced, though she was handing Mother her last jar of pickled peaches.

"She don't," Mrs. Wilcox piped up.

"I'm here strictly on church business."

"Strictly business," Mrs. Wilcox echoed. "And no funny business."

Mrs. Dowdel turned on Dad, who was fighting his way into his suit coat. "You can't get a church up and goin' without a good funeral first," she told him. "Any fool could tell you that. Without a funeral, you ain't got a chance in—"

"The world," Mrs. Wilcox said. "I haven't missed a funeral since the great flu epidemic. A good funeral makes the whole week go better."

"I want me one," Mrs. Dowdel said.

A grave silence fell over us. Was she talking about her

own funeral? Was she . . . planning ahead? Dad looked lost.

"And the . . . departed?" he asked, feeling his way.

"Oh well, shoot," Mrs. Dowdel said—expostulated. "I brought her with me."

Did she mean Mrs. Wilcox? Mrs. Wilcox stood there in Mrs. Dowdel's big shadow. A toothpick wavered out between two of her teeth. She didn't look ready to depart, quite.

But Mrs. Dowdel was sliding the box out of the crook of her arm. It was wrapped up in a piece of old rug or an Indian blanket, something ragged and sewed together with thongs. It was roped around, and there was some beadwork stuck on.

"I'm sick to death of all this fussin' and fumin' about restless spirits and floatin' princesses and all such horse—"

"Feathers," Mrs. Wilcox said. "That's right. Mrs. Dowdel's fixin' to get down to the end of her rope. And you don't want to rile her. She's about a squat jump away from—"

"I'll tell it, Effie," Mrs. Dowdel said. "I'm up to here with juvenile delinquent sorority gals and riffraff from out of town trampin' my property like they own it. This used to be a nice quiet little town. Now look at it."

"Just look," Mrs. Wilcox said.

"Ah," Dad said.

"So I dug her up," Mrs. Dowdel said. "That so-called Kickapoo Princess, and here she is."

She handed the box over, and it was in Dad's hands before he knew it. We stood there stunned. Mother went snow white. Phyllis just went. Ruth Ann was all eyes. She poked at the bridge of her nose like she was wearing spectacles.

"This is all I could find of her, and it's not much more than eye-teeth and gristle. But then, she'd been pushing up my melons for a good many years," Mrs. Dowdel said. "She wasn't nothin' but a bag of bones even before I was born. And I'm old as dirt."

"Older," Mrs. Wilcox murmured.

"I want a good church funeral for her so the public will know she's not adrift around the back of my place. And I want her buried out in the cemetery along with everybody else."

She was turning to go now and shooing Mrs. Wilcox to the door. "Do your best, Preacher," she said over her massive shoulder. "And do it up big. I'll get the word out. You get the lead out."

Then they were gone.

"Night now!" Mrs. Wilcox called back out of the evening. Dad stood there with all that remained of the Kickapoo Princess.

"I'm not a showman, Ellen," he said at last to Mother. "I'm no Gypsy Piggott. It sounds like they won't want a funeral. They'll want a show."

"You'll know what to do, Jack," Mother said. "You'll rise to the occasion. This may just be a heaven-sent opportunity for you."

She looked fairly sure, though it was hard to picture

Mrs. Dowdel as a messenger from heaven. But Mother may already have been thinking about sheet music and a choir. She'd met Dad when she was in the choir and he was in his first pulpit. You could almost hear hymns humming in her head.

Dad jiggled the box. The label on the blanket around it read:

MADE IN THE USA

PENDLETON, OREGON

"I don't think there's much of anything in this box," Dad said. "Or anybody."

"Maybe she's there in spirit," Mother said.

"Or maybe Mrs. Dowdel dreamed her up out of thin air," Dad said. "I'm not sure the truth is always in her."

But then they both noticed Ruth Ann right below them, all ears and as innocent as if she'd never worn a feathered headdress in all her six years.

CHAPTER EIGHT

Indian Summer

We laid the Kickapoo Princess to rest the Saturday before high school homecoming. It was a brilliant fall day with the sumac running riot in the hedgerows. Indian summer, in fact.

In a pinch we could pack forty people into the pews.

By mid-morning upward of two hundred people were standing outside. A press tent rose in the park. WGN from Chicago was broadcasting on live radio what they called The Final Rites of the Piatt County Pocahontas.

Mother was already at church. She'd called for a choir practice on Wednesday night, and eighty people turned out, though she could only field fourteen. Now people from Casner to Lovington remembered they were Methodists and came in waves. You wouldn't have been surprised to see them marching across the fields, singing "Onward, Christian Soldiers."

As the clock ticked toward two, Dad and I stood on our porch. His hand was on my shoulder, which I liked. Cars and trucks were parked past us out to Salt Crick. It was the first time I ever saw Dad wear his robe with the velvet down the front. There was a whiff of mothballs about him, and his upper lip was beady with sweat. This might have been when I first noticed it wasn't that easy being a grown-up.

"'I make myself a slave to everyone,'" he remarked, "'to win as many as possible.'"

"That's Scripture," I said to him. "Am I right, Dad?"

"I Corinthians. 9:19," he said.

"Dad, am I going to have to be a minister when I grow up?"

"If you hear the Call, you'll have to answer it."

"Oh," I said.

But then Dad said, thoughtful and far-off, "Or you may just want to let it ring."

Now Mrs. Dowdel was coming across her yard. Mrs. Wilcox and Ruth Ann bobbed behind, all aproned, all making for church. A fully feathered pheasant, stuffed, rode the front of Mrs. Dowdel's hat.

"Right nice day for a funeral," Mrs. Wilcox called over to us. "God's smilin'."

"He may be laughing out loud," Dad said, under his breath.

Mrs. Dowdel glanced over and seemed to see me for the first time in her life. "That your boy, Preacher?"

"It is," Dad called back. "And I believe that's one of my daughters trailing you."

Ruth Ann waved as onward they trooped, single-file into the gathering crowd.

In the distance the high school band started down the main street from the other way, playing "Nearer, My God, to Thee" in march time. The glitter on the majorettes' batons winked in the sun.

Dad squeezed my shoulder, here in this last moment.

I'd already been down to the church an hour before, trying to usher. But people had kept knocking me over to get in the pews. Mrs. Weidenbach had roped off an entire pew for the Daughters of the American Revolution, and she'd brought her own rope.

There were plenty of United Brethren there too, and everybody else. Wash-foot. Sprinklers and dunkers. Even some Amish over from Arthur in buggies. The Shellabarger sisters were sighted, Miss Cora and Miss Flora, and people said that Miss Cora hadn't been off their porch since before the Korean Police Action.

Dad and I turned up the street through the bright, swirling leaves. Switchy-tailed squirrels peered down from high branches to the heads below. The Veterans of Foreign Wars were selling pulled pork sandwiches out of a truck bed. The crowds parted, and everybody noticed Dad's robe. Up the rickety church steps we went, Dad and I.

The Methodist Women's Circle had placed the princess's box on a draped table below the pulpit. Around it was an artistic arrangement of fall leaves and asters. People had brought various souvenirs from trips out west on Route 66: clay pottery, sweetgrass baskets, toy totem poles, calabashes, two tomahawks.

Mrs. Dowdel had already elbowed three Daughters of the American Revolution out of the front pew to make room for herself, Mrs. Wilcox, and Ruth Ann.

The color guard of the American Legion pushed in past Dad and me. They were in their spit-and-polish blue with gold braid, bearing two flags: the Stars and Stripes and the State of Illinois.

The high school band members worked in behind them. In fact the whole high school, though I didn't see Phyllis. There were some notes clenched in Dad's hand as he started down the aisle. Mother's choir broke into "Once to Every Man and Nation Comes the Moment to Decide." All the plastic in the windows had blown out. Gold autumn light poured in, and a few bright leaves.

Dad turned at the front. He didn't climb up into the pulpit and put himself above the rest of us. As Mother often pointed out, he was modest to a fault.

Behind me a television camera from WSOY rolled in. Dad saw that. He pointed at the camera crew and in a ringing voice said, "Take that thing out of here. This is a place of worship." The crew fell back, and the congregation stirred. Dad looked somewhat surprised at himself.

There was sudden silence except for the wasps in the eaves.

"'Open your eyes and look at the fields!'" Dad intoned. "'They are ripe for harvest.'"

Mrs. Dowdel spoke up from the front pew. "John. 4:35."

The congregation craned and murmured. They'd never seen her in church.

Dad looked down at the table. Beside the princess's box was a piece of painted pottery, maybe ancient, probably not.

Dad held it up. "'We are the clay,'" he said, looking to heaven through the breaks in the roof. "'You are the potter.'"

"Isaiah. 64:8," Mrs. Dowdel responded.

"We're here to remember those who came before us," Dad said in his regular voice. "The stewards of this land that now we till, the place where we make our homes and build our lives and hold our children in our arms."

The congregation edged forward. He had a fine voice, Dad did. They could tell he was a thoughtful man, and now they heard his thoughts, about how people, families, had always lived here. How we were links in the chain.

It wasn't a long sermon, and the congregation stayed with him every word of the way. He hadn't mentioned the Kickapoo Princess, the Piatt County Pocahontas. Maybe people forgot why they'd come.

But then as he drew to a close, Dad put his hand on the princess's box, and people stood up at the back, just to see his hand there.

And Dad said,

> *She was a child of these prairies,*
> *Under these blue skies above,*
> *And work-worn hands long forgotten*
> *Buried her here, with love.*

People stopped fanning themselves with the funeral home fans.

> *The creatures of ditch and burrow*
> *Gave her pelts to keep winter out;*
> *The meandering streams and rivers*
> *Gave her drink in the times of drought.*
>
> *Her church was the sighing forest,*
> *Her text was the endless plain,*
> *Her communion the juice of the berry*
> *And the loaf from this Illinois grain.*
>
> *How lightly her people lived here*
> *In the seasons' ebb and flow;*

May we leave this land as lovely
When it's our own time to go.

A stillness stirred inside every soul within these rickety walls.

"Amen," Mrs. Dowdel said into the quiet. "Amen to that." And from this golden Indian summer day, we had us a church.

CHAPTER NINE

Homecoming Day, and Night

We buried the princess's box in among the roots of a sugar maple at the edge of the cemetery. From there she'd have a view across open country to the Sangamon River bottoms.

At the Sunday service next day it took four ushers to pass the plates along the crowded pews. And while rich old Miss Cora and Miss Flora Shellabarger didn't attend, they sent a fifty-dollar check on the Weidenbach bank for the church roof fund.

School was okay too, more or less. They were letting me live. But even if I hadn't been a preacher's kid, all the groups were already set up. Farm kids. Town kids. Then there was me. The farm kids ate at their own picnic table at lunch. But one of them turned out to be a pretty good guy. He was a big old raw-boned country boy named Jess Wood.

He was twice my size, but he seemed to be making his first run at sixth grade. And he didn't like bullies. One noon he happened to notice that big Newt Fluke was stealing my lunch and passing it to Elmo Leaper, Jr. They were absent a lot, but when they weren't, I went hungry. I'd already tried grabbing my lunch back from Newt, and I'd got a fat lip out of it. And no lunch.

On this particular noon I was already going for the apple in my desk when Jess Wood climbed off the farmers' picnic table and ambled over.

"Hand it back, Newt," he said in Newt Fluke's face.

"Why would I do a thing like that?" Newt's voice had changed, probably many semesters ago.

"Because I might have a word with your leader, Roscoe Burdick."

At mere mention of Roscoe Burdick, Elmo Leaper, Jr., pulled back and jammed his mitts in his bib overalls. Newt was left holding the lunch. "What's Roscoe Burdick got to do with anything?" said Newt, shifty-eyed.

"This kid is Phyllis Barnhart's kid brother, you wing nut," Jess said, like it explained everything.

Newt blinked, and my lunch seemed to grow heavy in his hand. "Who says it's your business, rube?" he said to Jess, though his voice cracked.

"Jess says," I piped. My hands were on my hips because now I had backup. I don't know what came over me. I could have got myself smeared all over the room.

"Easy, partner," Jess said to me out of the corner of his mouth. "*These* say it's my business," he said to Newt. Jess made his farmer hands into fists.

"Eat up," Newt said to me, and dropped my lunch on my desk. Egg salad on whole wheat.

"Thanks," I mumbled to Jess.

"Anytime," he said loud enough for Newt to hear.

I wasn't sure what had happened. Phyllis and . . . Roscoe Burdick? I sort of knew she wasn't going to committee meetings when she went out every other night. But did I know *this*? My head buzzed.

And how in the dickens did this big old country boy Jess even know about Roscoe Burdick and Phyllis anyway?

Because everybody around here knew everything. Everybody but me. Jess ambled on back to his group. They stuck together and cut out right after school to do chores.

Phyllis wasn't complaining these days as much as you'd think. I never saw her at school, of course, and she never came looking for me. But everybody on the high school side was getting worked up about homecoming.

Phyllis seemed to be out at a committee meeting most nights. She naturally wouldn't be riding on the Iota Nu Beta float because she'd made an enemy out of Waynetta Blalock. But this didn't appear to faze her. Mother thought Phyllis was beginning to settle in.

But then on Wednesday she dug in her heels and wouldn't

go to school. Ruth Ann came down to breakfast, bright-eyed and bushytailed, to say Phyllis was in bed for the day.

"Oh dear," Mother said. "Do you think she's running a temperature?"

"Nope." Ruth Ann tweaked the ribbons on her braids.

"Is she looking pale and washed out?"

"She always looks pale and washed out without her lipstick on." Ruth Ann made big eyes. She actually only had two expressions: worried and wide-eyed.

Mother was at the drainboard, pouring the cream off the top of the milk. She turned. "Ruth Ann, honey, Phyllis doesn't wear lipstick. She's only f—"

"Not at *home*," Ruth Ann said. "She waits till she gets to school."

This was true. But I wouldn't have told it because I'm not a snitch. Also, if I'd ratted on her, she'd have nuked me into next November.

At the drainboard Mother took some deep, calming breaths. "Does Phyllis say why she isn't going to school today?"

Ruth Ann beamed. She was a first grader with the answer. "Elvis. They're shipping him out to Germany today. The army is. Phyllis says she can't be expected to concentrate on anything else." Ruth Ann scanned Mother to see how she took this. "Phyllis says she's in mourning for her life."

Mother made a tight little ball of the dish rag and gazed away out the window.

Phyllis had been writing Elvis Presley right along since he'd been drafted into the army last winter. I didn't see any difference between writing him at Fort Hood, Texas, and writing him in Germany. He never answered anyway. I couldn't follow Phyllis's thinking, and it might have been because I was a boy.

Anyway, after sulking in bed till after school, Phyllis was up that night in time for a committee meeting about the Future Farmers of America hayride. Though I thought the Future Farmers hayride had already happened.

Then before you knew it, it was Saturday and nearly noon. From the other end of town the band was tuning up on the high school blacktop. The homecoming parade was a bigger deal than the game itself. People had been stuffing tissue paper into chicken wire floats all week.

You wouldn't expect Mrs. Dowdel to take much interest. She hated noise and hadn't gone to high school. Besides, she and Ruth Ann were busy as bird dogs. They'd plucked all the geese Mrs. Dowdel had shot, for restuffing pillows.

But in fact Mrs. Dowdel loved a parade and never missed one. She and Ruth Ann were setting up a picnic out front just a ditch away from the parade route. And though Mrs. Dowdel didn't neighbor, we Barnharts were invited.

She and Ruth Ann were back and forth from kitchen to road, bringing deviled eggs, pea salad, stuffed celery.

Somehow I got pulled into it and sent to the cobhouse for folding chairs.

"Bring extry," Mrs. Dowdel told me. "You never know."

It was a day's work finding anything in that cobhouse. The whole place smelled like olden times: cider and neat's-foot oil, and at one time there must have been a cat. A brace of dead, naked geese hung from the beams, plucked and singed and waiting to be melted down for grease. Big, swaying bags of goose down hung in my way. Every floorboard was loose. This was another likely spot where Mrs. Dowdel might have stashed her money.

You never saw such a raft of stuff. Traps and tackle and a shingle machine. Ruth Ann's hula hoop hung from a nail since she didn't have time for it anymore. I finally dug out the folding chairs, all stenciled: PROPERTY OF THE SHELBYVILLE PARK DIST.

Then we were settled out by the ditch, around Mrs. Dowdel: Mother and Ruth Ann and I. Mrs. Dowdel's big knees were wide-spread with her apron stretched drum-tight under her paper plate. Dad was to ride in the parade with the seven other preachers of the Council of Churches. We supposed Phyllis would be in the parade too, somewhere. It was an unusual sight—Mother right there next to Mrs. Dowdel.

She overflowed two folding chairs. Nudging Mother,

she said, "I worked to get all the buckshot out of this goose." She waved a sandwich. "But watch where you chew. Bite down hard on that shot, and you could bust up your choppers."

Mother looked at her sliced goose sandwich.

"I haul off and roast a goose till the skin's crispy and it's fallin' off the bone," Mrs. Dowdel explained. "And I stick a fork in it so the fat will run off. You want your goose loose. Then I'll stuff it with prunes. Never pass up a chance at a prune." She nudged Ruth Ann on her other side. "This girl and I has plucked all the geese, and there'll be down enough left over for you folks's pillows. Then we'll go to work and melt down the carcasses we don't eat for goose grease and add us some camphor to rub on your chest, come winter."

Mother took a quick look down at her own chest.

"We eat and wear and sleep on the goose." Mrs. Dowdel tapped Mother's knee. "Give me a good goose every time."

Ruth Ann looked around her. "Me too," she piped. "Every time."

Now we saw the revolving light on top of Police Chief C. P. Snokes's Dodge, clearing the street. Right about then, here came Mrs. Wilcox, wearing carpet slippers, stumping along the slab in her hat and veil and Mackinaw jacket.

"Hoo-boy, here comes Effie," Mrs. Dowdel remarked.

"She can smell a free lunch from here to Sunday. And you think she's bowlegged now. You should have seen her as a girl. She'd try to cross her legs and miss."

Mother swallowed hard, and the band came high-stepping along, blaring a medley of fight song and "God Bless America." The fight song was the same, though they'd changed the name of the team from "Fightin' Farmers" to "Kickapoo Kickers."

Glitter batons spun in the treetops, but the majorettes were second string because Vanette Pankey and Bonnie Burhoops would be riding the homecoming queen's float.

An old Hupmobile sedan, about a 1932 model, rolled by, draped in bunting. It was the Daughters of the American Revolution, all seven of them shoehorned in with Mrs. L. J. Weidenbach at the wheel. Then a big wooden-sided wagon, horse-drawn, with the corn-husking team. Corn husking was a competitive sport around here. Then an antique La France hook and ladder truck.

All the preachers of the Council of Churches were divided into a pair of Bel-Air convertibles, courtesy of the Chevrolet agency in Monticello. Dad waved at us from between two United Brethren. The other preachers were showing Dad some respect now. He sat tall among them, looking good. My dad. We waved back.

The varsity team followed, sheepish and suited up on the seat backs of a line of Pontiac Catalinas. Then the Future

Farmers hay frame, then the Home Ec Club. We looked on every float for Phyllis but didn't see her.

Mrs. Wilcox had settled just back of Mrs. Dowdel's elbow. She'd propped up her veil and was working over a plate of sliced goose and baked beans.

The excitement mounted as the big float with the homecoming court came into view, drawn by a factory-fresh John Deere tractor. Applause rippled off the porches all up the street. There on the high throne sat the Homecoming Queen surrounded by her court, all wearing dress-up suits, mum corsages, and high-heeled shoes. At the queen's feet, representing the freshmen, was Barbara Jean Jeeter. She was sitting kind of careful on one haunch. Flanking the queen were Edna-Earl Stubbs for the sophomores, Bonnie Burhoops for the juniors, and Vanette Pankey for the seniors. They all happened to be Iota Nu Betas, though sororities weren't allowed. Nobody quite remembered electing Waynetta Blalock as Homecoming Queen. It was just a done deal.

"Whozatt hard-faced gal?" Mrs. Dowdel asked, pointing a stuffed celery stalk up at Waynetta, high and mighty on her throne. Her rhinestone tiara rode her blinding, flame-red locks.

Mrs. Wilcox squinted up. "It's Waynetta, Carleen Lovejoy's girl."

"She looks a little peaked and off her feed," Mrs. Dowdel observed. "And I've seen better hair on bacon."

Mother choked.

It was tradition that each girl on the float be attended by her boyfriend or some guy from her class. But Waynetta had ruled all boys off the float because her boyfriend didn't go to high school and wasn't available. The whole school knew this. Ruth Ann knew this. No boys because Waynetta said so.

She'd been smirking from side to side right through town, but Mrs. Dowdel's was the last house before the open fields.

Slowly, Waynetta turned and deigned to look down upon us. Real slow, though I doubt if she looked Mrs. Dowdel in the eye.

There was something up there in Waynetta's lap. You'd expect a spray of American Beauty roses, something like that. But no. It was a small, weird shape nestled up there. And bald. And one-eyed. It was a doll, loved to baldness with but a single working eye. Waynetta held it out for us to see.

"Grachel!" Ruth Ann screamed, flying off her folding chair. Her picnic went everywhere. "GIMME BACK GRACHEL!"

It was Ruth Ann's long-lost doll, so she hadn't gone home to Terre Haute after all.

With a casual gesture, Waynetta pitched Grachel into the air. She turned in the afternoon, arms out, and lit in the ditch. Ruth Ann lunged.

In a voice way too tough for a Homecoming Queen, Waynetta hollered out, "And tell Phyllis Barnhart to keep her thieving hands off my man, or she'll end up in the ditch herself, and I'll see to it personally. *And* I'll black both her eyes. I knew she was trouble the minute I laid eyes on her."

Her court seemed to go along with it. Vanette Pankey nodded down at us, saying, "She means it."

Waynetta adjusted her tiara, and the parade lurched past us. It rolled on out into the countryside to disband. Dust settled.

I thought it was pretty lowdown, picking on a little kid and stealing her doll because you didn't like her big sister. So I was in the ditch, helping Ruth Ann fish Grachel out of some standing water. Ruth Ann was crying, partly from relief. But also because somebody was nasty enough to kidnap Grachel.

"But what did all that mean?" Mother said, completely baffled.

I had a hazy idea, though I wasn't a hundred percent.

Mrs. Dowdel said nothing but "Hoo-boy."

"You can say that again," Mrs. Wilcox said.

Phyllis swung home for a quick supper with us that evening. We hadn't seen her in the parade because, as she said, she'd been back at school on the clean-up committee. Though she never cleaned up anything around home, including her own room.

Then in a pair of fresh socks, she was heading for the door and the sock hop down at the gym. Mother thought it was all right because teachers would be there to chaperone. "But be back by ten," Mother called after her. "You're only f—"

"Don't wait up," Phyllis yelled as the door banged behind her.

The rest of us had a quiet night at home. Fairly quiet. These nights there were always people out in Mrs. Dowdel's melon patch, many with lanterns and all with spades, digging. They were the ones who believed she'd buried her money in her patch. Mrs. Dowdel let them think it. Her crops were all in, and the ground needed a good digging over before winter anyway. All she did was serve notice on the world that she'd be out in her patch on Halloween night in case of funny business. So bear it in mind.

It was all hours when a pounding came on our front door. Mother was still awake because Phyllis wasn't home yet. She started down the stairs and stopped.

"Jack, get up and get dressed," she called in to Dad. "I'm afraid it's Mrs. Dowdel."

Now I was up and trailing Mother downstairs. Only Ruth Ann slept through this. She and Grachel were tucked up in bed, sawing logs.

Out on the porch the discs of Mrs. Dowdel's spectacles flashed in the ceiling light. Mother fumbled the door open, and we saw someone else. Not Mrs. Wilcox. It was another small gnome of a figure—one more ancient lady in a town full of them. She wore old-fashioned metal curlers in her sparse hair and a fur coat. White cold cream clung in all the crevices of her face. I almost knew her.

Mother wavered on the doorsill.

"This here's Cora Shellabarger." Mrs. Dowdel pointed out the small figure sagging in her shadow. She was one of the Shellabarger sisters, the richest old maids in town. "She come to me about it instead of heading directly to you folks."

Miss Cora Shellabarger seemed to whimper. "Well, it's not the kind of thing you want to bring to the preacher, of all people."

"Everybody brings everything to my door," Mrs. Dowdel proclaimed. "I'm the town dump." She elbowed Miss Shellabarger. "Go ahead and tell 'em, Cora. Spit it out and shuck right down to the cob."

Miss Shellabarger worked her hands. "I wish Flora had come in place of me," she murmured. "It's about your girl, Mrs. Barnhart, your daughter Phyllis. She's breathing, and she's conscious, and she's on the settee in our front room. And I don't want you to worry because we think she'll live."

CHAPTER TEN

One Too Many

The Shellabarger place was known for miles around. Abraham Lincoln had slept in the milk house on his way to Bement. That was when the milk house was a log dwelling. Old Man Shellabarger had built the present structure in 1878, with gingerbread porches and a tower as tall as a silo.

The Pickle had gas in it now, but Dad never thought to drive. We ran all the way, kicking through the leaves of the sleeping town. At the Shellabargers', the porch light lit the yard.

A car was piled up at the foot of the front steps. It had swerved off the road, jumped the ditch, bounced off the mounting block, and plowed a furrow across the lawn. A car door was off and over in a flowerbed. The frame was way out of whack. The car was scrap iron now and hadn't been worth much even before it tried to climb the Shellabargers' front steps. An old DeSoto, with mud flaps and a pair of squirrel tails. One-eyed as I recalled it, with a slipping clutch and a Hollywood muffler. The taillights were still on, but the driver was long gone.

We hit the porch steps at a gallop. Miss Flora Shellabarger swung open the tall front doors.

Phyllis was on a settee in the big, shadowy front room. She had an ice pack on her head and both eyes were already black. Her skirt was ripped, and her sock hop socks weren't so fresh now. She looked pale and washed out, even with lipstick on. The minute she saw Mother and Dad, she felt a lot worse and fell back, clutching her head carefully.

Mother and Dad moved up on her. They checked her over and felt her head under the ice pack. They lifted her chin and examined her black eyes. She looked like a somewhat dazed muskrat, in barrettes.

Mother looked long and hard at her. "Sock hop?" Mother said. Phyllis shrank, though only a little.

Mrs. Dowdel and Miss Cora Shellabarger barged in behind us. They'd fallen back in the dash across town. Mrs. Dowdel could have kept up, but Miss Cora was wearing yarn house slippers, with pompoms.

Mrs. Dowdel filled up every space, even this vast room. She lifted her nose, and her specs gleamed. "What's that smell?" she inquired. Miss Flora stiffened. There were a lot of smells. It was the eighty-year-old house of a couple of eighty-year-old women.

"Smells like a brewery," Mrs. Dowdel observed. "I wouldn't say no to a Miller High Life myself, after that sprint across town."

"Well, I never!" Miss Flora yanked her bathrobe ties tight. "Mrs. Dowdel, I'll have you to know Papa was teetotal and Mama was a founding member of the Women's Christian Temperance Union. I myself turned down a perfectly good offer of marriage from a man because he drank."

"Orville Butz," Mrs. Dowdel recalled.

"Never you mind who it was," Miss Flora snapped, cutting short the local history. "Liquor never crossed our threshold. This is a Methodist home."

Miss Flora was a lot feistier than Miss Cora, but Mrs. Dowdel waved her away. "I'm talkin' about that girl right there." She pointed past us at Phyllis, growing smaller on the settee. "She's had one too many."

Silence fell hard. The mantelpiece clock ticked off several slow seconds.

Then Mother turned on me, of all people. "Bob, go straight home," she said. "In our haste, we've forgotten about Ruth Ann left all alone. Cut right along in case she wakes up."

I held my ground. I wanted to know what would happen next. I was all ears.

"Bob, go now," Mother said. So I had to, which I didn't think was fair. Ruth Ann was sawing logs and slept like one. Anyway, they were just trying to get rid of me. Dad pointed out the door.

But in the long run, it didn't matter. I heard all about it. Who didn't? Grade school kids, hermits, the hard-of-hearing. Everybody. As a rule, Miss Cora and Miss Flora would have been the last to know. But this had happened on their doorstep and knocked them out of bed.

No story moves faster than the one about the bad boy and the preacher's daughter. You could pick up six or eight versions at the Dairy Queen alone. But where to begin? Might as well start with the car, the one-eyed DeSoto.

When he had it towed, Police Chief C. P. Snokes noted that it wasn't registered to anybody. That meant it was the Burdicks'. Anything missing throughout the county from a handsaw to a corncrib ended up at the Burdicks'. Besides, everybody knew the driver was Roscoe Burdick, blue-and-green-eyed Roscoe Burdick, who'd welcomed me to town by half drowning me, then hanging me out to dry in the Dowdel privy. *That* Roscoe Burdick.

He was at the wheel and drunk as a skunk when he lost control of the DeSoto on homecoming night and plowed that furrow up to the Shellabarger porch steps. Phyllis flew out, lighting headfirst on that first concrete step.

But how she happened to be there and not at the sock hop made for a longer story.

First of all, Roscoe Burdick had sideburns down to here and shirts unbuttoned down to there. He seemed to know all the verses of the song "Ready Teddy," and he owned a pair of blue suede shoes. He was about as Elvis as Phyllis would ever get.

Waynetta Blalock had always thought she had Roscoe pretty well sewed up. She'd told the whole high school that she could make something out of him, Burdick or not. Waynetta's mother naturally wouldn't let a Burdick on the porch. But that only made Roscoe more interesting to Waynetta. Her plan was to graduate and then start to look seriously at silver patterns.

But from that night before school started when Roscoe saw Phyllis strolling past the Dairy Queen, it was a whole new ballgame.

Of course he was pushing twenty, but that's the age Phyllis thought she was, in her head. She'd been sneaking out with him all fall.

They'd been spotted at a tractor pull as far away as Rantoul. In fact on homecoming sock hop night he'd taken her over to the Decatur Drive-in to see an Elvis double feature, *Loving You* and *King Creole*. We'd been peppered with clues all fall, but Mother and Dad didn't pick up on them since Phyllis was only fourteen.

Waynetta had, of course. She'd been sitting home with

nobody to sneak out with and getting ready to blow her top. So in time I guess she *would* have blacked both Phyllis's eyes if the porch steps hadn't done it for her.

On Sunday Mother meant to drag Phyllis out of bed and make her go to church to show her shameful face to the world. But Phyllis threw up right at her. Oh boy, was she sick, all day. "I thought it was root beer," she groaned, but got no sympathy.

"If I believed this would teach you a lesson, young lady," Mother said, "I'd be happier than I am."

I was sent up with Sunday dinner on a tray: liver and onions, pickled beets, and vinegar slaw. Their smell and the stomach-pink walls of Phyllis's room were a bad combination. She was sick all over again.

I edged the tray onto her bed, just trying to be helpful.

"I'll never eat again," she said from deep in her damp pillow. "Take it away."

"Where'll I put it?"

"Don't make me tell you."

"Mother and Dad say we may have to leave town, thanks to you," I pointed out to her. "They say we haven't set a good example for the community and all eyes are upon us. Also, liquor was involved."

"I thought it was root beer," Phyllis moaned.

"You said that," I answered.

"If those two old biddies, those Shellabarger sisters,

would just keep their traps shut, we could forget all about it," Phyllis said. "But they won't."

"Also, liquor was involved," I reminded.

"And that old battle-ax Mrs. Dowdel is everywhere I turn," Phyllis griped. "She's all over me like . . . like . . ."

"White on rice," I said.

"Like what?" Phyllis groaned.

"White on rice. It's one of her sayings."

"I hate this podunk town," Phyllis said. "I can't tell you how much. And Mother and Dad are prejudiced against Roscoe. Everybody is. Nobody understands him."

"Everybody understands he cut and ran when he piled up the car and left you knocked cuckoo on the Shellabarger steps," I remarked.

"He's sensitive." Phyllis gagged, reaching for the basin. "All he needs is the love of a good woman." Then she was real sick again.

On Monday morning Phyllis, wearing sunglasses, clung to her mattress and said she wouldn't be going to school, ever. She was resigning from freshman year because Waynetta Blalock was prejudiced against her and so was the whole school.

From the foot of her bed Mother was telling her about how she'd be going to school and nowhere else. Phyllis just might be grounded for life. You never saw Mother lose her temper.

It was against her beliefs. But she was blowing sky-high this morning. She had a good grip on Phyllis's bed railing.

"Young lady," she said, "I don't know what sort of phase you're going through. And I certainly can't remember going through anything like it myself, thank goodness. But I'll tell you here and now you've gone too far, and I'm going to nip you in the bud."

Even I shied at that, out here in the hall. Phyllis didn't.

"Are you threatening me?" she snapped from the bed. The covers were pulled up to her chin. She was all sunglasses and sassy mouth.

"I am giving you fair warning," Mother said in a low and steady voice. "I will take steps."

Ruth Ann and Grachel sat on their bed over across the pink stripe. Their three eyes took everything in.

I'd only lingered a little at the door, on my way to school. But Mother saw me with the eyes in the back of her head. She turned on me, of all people.

"Bob!"

I froze.

"Just how much of this whole . . . situation did you know about, young man?"

Silence fell. Mother waited, her back still turned to me. Three eyes turned on me from Ruth Ann's bed. "I'm waiting," Mother said.

"Not too much," I mumbled. "Just what everybody knows at school. Even the country kids. Just stuff. Like how

Roscoe and Phyllis were spotted at the tractor pull over in Rantoul. And she goes on a lot of hay rides, not just the Future Farmers one. And of course everybody knows Waynetta Blalock is real sore at Phyllis for steal—"

"ALL RIGHT, ALL RIGHT. I'M GOING." Phyllis flung off her covers and staggered blindly out of bed in her sunglasses. And off she sulked to school in a darned skirt and still looking a lot like a muskrat. Or a raccoon. Whichever one has big black eyes.

CHAPTER ELEVEN

Blazing Pumpkin

With homecoming behind us, Halloween began to happen, two weeks early. Soaped windows and pinned car horns and lawn furniture up in trees and dead cats on porches. Unknown hands put a brooder house, complete with a flock of hens inside, on the railroad tracks. The Norfolk & Western evening St. Louis train hit it broadside. There was kindling and chicken parts on every roof in town. Trees dripped giblets, and there was hen grit everywhere.

Halloween began early, but then so did Mrs. Dowdel. When it came to the future, she was always a step ahead.

There were two schools of thought about her. One was that greasing her porch steps or tearing down her privy wasn't a real good idea. On the other hand, nobody had yet dug up her treasure of cash money, wherever it was buried. As usual, she seemed to pay no heed to public opinion.

She and Ruth Ann even carved a giant pumpkin. They'd scooped it out, baked some pies and a few loaves of pumpkin bread. Now it stood blazing with candles every night on the Dowdel front steps, daring anybody to knock it off.

On Halloween night Dad took Ruth Ann out to ring a few doorbells and collect some treats. He had calls to pay on shut-ins anyway. For a costume Ruth Ann wanted to go as an Indian princess, but Dad talked her out of it. In the end, she came downstairs with her trick-or-treat sack, wearing a plaid flannel shirt of mine, her own bedroom slippers, and one of Mother's hats, with a veil.

"Honey, who are you?" Dad said.

"Mrs. Wilcox," she said, crossing her eyes.

They left, and I went on up to the party at the Grange Hall the 4-H gave to keep us off the streets. It was an okay party, with donuts. At least we didn't have to pin the tail on the donkey or bob for apples. Some of the country kids came in for it. I guess you can't do much Halloweening down on the farm.

Jess Wood showed up, and there was some corn silk smoked outside behind the trucks. But a few of the eighth graders started a game that could have ended up with kissing, so a bunch of us went home. Jess did, and he could drive his dad's truck himself.

Later that night there was a thumbnail of moon, a touch of winter in the hazy air. Phyllis and Ruth Ann were both in bed. Phyllis hadn't gone anywhere, being grounded.

Ruth Ann had laid out all the treats she'd collected to show Grachel. Now she was sawing logs. I was at my window, still dressed from the party, waiting for whatever would happen next. Something was going to. You could feel it in the air.

The giant pumpkin glowed on Mrs. Dowdel's front steps. Above the cobhouse roof hung the glow of a campfire dying down. Anyone trespassing on her melon patch would see a figure humped in afghans, a shotgun across her knees, sitting guard as promised.

Car horns still went off, but far away. Sudden gunfire from right next door would have come as no surprise, of course. It was like Fort Leonard Wood over there. But all was silence until the sudden snap of a kitchen door.

A cloud blurred the narrow moon. A large figure crossed the side yard, darker than night except for the white hair.

I was downstairs when Dad opened the door. Mrs. Dowdel was on the porch. But how could she be since she was sitting guard out in her melon patch?

But here she was, dressed in a complete outfit saved from her dead husband: canvas coat over overalls, gum boots, flap cap—hunting gear.

"Bagged him," she said to Dad. "Call the law."

We had a phone now. We had to. People kept calling up Dad to plan their future funerals. When he turned back to make the call, I slipped out. After all, an old lady shouldn't be out at all hours, alone in the dark.

The corners of her dim kitchen were crowded with eerie

shapes like severed heads: pumpkins too ugly to sell she was saving for Thanksgiving pies. "Don't worry," she said over her shoulder. "I got him tied to the leg of the bed."

I kept on her heels up the linoleum steps. Her heavy tread rocked the house. Light fell from one of the bedrooms—her grandson's: Joey's.

She filled the doorway, and somebody in there yelped at another sight of her.

"Turn me loose," a deep, whiny voice said. "I was just trick-or-treatin' is all I was doin'."

"With a crowbar and an ax in my upstairs bedroom?" she thundered. "You're lookin' at doin' time, boy, in the state reformatory." The gun hung broken over her canvas sleeve.

My heart thudded. Had she nailed him? Had he walked right into her trap through her unlocked front door past her blazing pumpkin? Had she finally got the goods on Roscoe Burdick?

I peered around her. There, kicking the bedroom floor on a rag rug between a crowbar and an ax—there with his wrists trussed up behind him and one ankle tied by fishing line to the leg of the bed, was Newt Fluke.

My heart sank.

Mrs. Dowdel had been gunning for Roscoe Burdick. But she'd bagged a Fluke. "Who sent you on this particular errand?"

"Nobody," he muttered. "I thought it up my own self."

"You ain't had a thought of your own yet," she remarked.

"And you know what you are?" Newt Fluke dared say from the floor, though his teeth chattered. There was no heat up here. "You're a durned witch. How can you be out in your melon patch *and* up here, settin' on this bed waitin' for me? How can you be in two places at once? You're a—"

"Boy," she said, "I can be in three places if need be."

Right about then we heard the siren on C. P. Snokes's Dodge. I'd kept behind Mrs. Dowdel, trying to be invisible in case Newt ever got out on bail.

I was home then, before I was missed. From my window I watched C. P. Snokes cramming Newt Fluke into the backseat of the squad car.

Mrs. Dowdel stood in the headlight glare with her fists on her big hips. She looked about half satisfied. Then when the car door closed on Newt, she said to the police chief, "They's another one in my snowballs." She crooked a thumb at her house. Sure enough, another gangly figure exploded out of the snowball bushes by her bay window. He swerved for the road, lighting out for tall timber. They let him go. Around here, you can run, but you can't hide. It was Elmo Leaper, Jr. He'd been left to stand guard while Newt went in to dig up the bedroom floor.

Halloween was finally petering out as the Dodge reversed into the road. I could hear Dad up in his attic study, trying to get back to his sermon. It might be Saturday already.

Then came a stealthy footfall on the stairs. I cracked my

door. Was Phyllis making a break for freedom? But it was Mother.

Mother, coming up, taking steps. I blinked to be sure. She looked kind of frost-bitten, though she was wearing several afghans. Weirder still, she carried a shotgun broken open over her arm. I couldn't believe my eyes. Mother? Packing heat? Silent as snow she made for her room, and the door closed behind her.

Mother and Mrs. Dowdel . . . working hand in glove? I fell back on the bed, dizzy with what grown-ups can get up to. I drifted off into my usual dream. The one about going down for the third time in Salt Crick, sucking brown water and dragonflies, with Roscoe Burdick's heavy hand on my head. But then I slept deeper than the crick, into November.

E'er the Winter
Storms Begin

CHAPTER TWELVE

Come, Ye Thankful People, Come

Thanksgiving now, and Christmas coming. The last leaves burned in long piles in the ditches. White smoke rose through bare limbs like ancient Kickapoo campfires.

The second frost had killed the cannas, so there was nothing between us and Mrs. Dowdel.

She was too busy to sit down. "Busier than a one-armed paperhanger," she claimed. "I'll die standing up, like an old ox," she said, another of her sayings.

She and Ruth Ann had made up little packets of suet to hang in the trees of the yard for the winter birds, the chickadees and cardinals. They tied them up in red and green ribbons, like Christmas presents coming early.

Now they were running a big lawn roller from somewhere, back and forth to hull the black walnuts carpeting her yard. Walnuts for cookies to come. They'd cut the sage and hung it in bunches from the cobhouse beams, for Thanksgiving dressing. In her kitchen, wherever the pumpkins weren't, were big dough bowls of bread crumbs, drying.

For their yard work, Mrs. Dowdel wore a pair of old cotton stockings pulled over her canvas coat sleeves, to keep out the draft. Ruth Ann was apt to burst into song while they worked. "Jesus Wants Me for a Sunbeam" and "We Gather Together to Ask the Lord's Blessing."

At school there was a lot of talk about pilgrims, but then there always was, this time of year. Mrs. Weidenbach, the banker's wife, came to our class to tell about how either she or one of her ancestors had come over on the *Mayflower*.

One thing I gave thanks for was that Newt Fluke had been taken out of sixth grade. He wasn't doing time, even though Mrs. Dowdel had caught him red-handed. Instead, the coach, who was also the high school principal, promoted Newt to freshman year so he could play out the football season. The coach planned to build a new ground offense around him.

And without Newt, Elmo Leaper, Jr., wasn't much. In fact he was kind of lonely. He came over to me one noon and said, "You wanna swap lunches?" He held up his bucket.

"Mine's peanut butter and grape jelly on Wonder Bread."

And I did because mine was corned beef and carrot sticks.

For a preacher's family Thanksgiving is all about feeding the hungry. Mother and the Methodist Women's Circle used the church as a gathering place for the food donations.

The church had new, top-of-the-line windows now, combination storms and screens.

Moore's IGA store donated turkeys, and the DAR brought canned goods. Mrs. Weidenbach herself promised her famous candied yams. I had to beg various stores for boxes to pack the dinners in because we'd be delivering them to shut-ins.

Though Mrs. Dowdel was no church woman, she was in and out all Thanksgiving week, gradually taking over the entire Methodist Feed the Hungry Thanksgiving Campaign. She was everywhere Mother turned.

"Who's baking them turkeys for you?" she demanded to know. When she heard it was Mrs. Pensinger, she said, "Reba Pensinger? Her turkey's dry as the bottom of a canary cage, and you could lubricate your car with her pan gravy. I'll do the birds in my oven. Have this boy bring them to the house." Meaning me.

Also, she thought very little of cranberry sauce in a can. "I wouldn't slop hogs with it. You can taste the can." A cauldron of bubbling, popping cranberries and orange peel seethed on her stove top, spiced with cinnamon sticks. As soon as school was over every afternoon, Ruth Ann stood on a kitchen chair and stirred.

Since Mrs. Pensinger didn't need oven space for the turkeys, she baked two or three pumpkin pies and brought them over to the church. But she said her pumpkins had let her down and all the good ones had vanished from her patch. Mrs. Dowdel baked twenty pumpkin pies at least. She showed Ruth Ann how to roll out dough and how to keep a bottom crust from getting soggy in the middle. Three mountains of dressing grew in her kitchen: chestnut, oyster, and cornbread.

The Methodist men volunteered to deliver the dinners on Thanksgiving Day. Broshear's Funeral Home offered their hearse. But Dad thought it might send the wrong message to people who saw it turning in at their place.

Somehow Mrs. Dowdel was in our car with us when we headed out. She hadn't dressed up. She wore her kitchen apron under her hunting jacket. Ruth Ann was in the backseat with her, also aproned. Dad was behind the wheel, and I sat beside him, where I liked to be. The whole Pickle smelled like turkey and cranberries and baked-this-morning Parker House rolls. Mrs. Dowdel gave us the directions to Aunt Madge's house, whoever she was. Mrs. Dowdel had been particular about us calling on Aunt Madge.

"Who is she anyway?" Ruth Ann wanted to know. "Is she a poor old widow woman?"

"Well, she's poor all right, and old as the hills." Mrs. Dowdel pondered. "Though I don't know as you could call her a widow woman. Nobody in that family ever got around to marrying."

"Then is she an old maid?" Ruth Ann inquired.

"Well, I don't know as you could call her that either," Mrs. Dowdel muttered.

Dad was all ears for whatever he could hear from up front. We spun along a county road through the frosty fields. I watched him work through the gears on the Pickle. He was inclined to ride the clutch a little. Mrs. Dowdel reached up to poke his shoulder. "Make a left at that Burma-Shave sign, Preacher."

We were about five miles out now and getting down to one lane, then a track, then two ruts. Up a turning was what looked like a large junkyard, and the fence was down. "Turn up that lane," Mrs. Dowdel directed, and Dad geared down.

The house itself lurked low, and the roof was patched with Coca-Cola signs. We all helped to carry Aunt Madge's Thanksgiving dinner. "Go on in," Mrs. Dowdel said. "She don't lock up."

Inside was a lot like outside and somewhat colder. You could see your breath. Dad had to duck in the doorway.

The floor wasn't all there. Then over by a stove a pile of rags became an old, old woman in a La-Z-Boy recliner.

"Hoo-boy," Ruth Ann whispered. "That's the oldest-looking woman I ever saw."

Mrs. Dowdel nodded. "She was only about three years behind me in school."

We had to clear a plank table to put down the boxes of dinner.

The old, old woman noticed us. She had a long red nose she kept wiping with a matching bandanna. "Get off my place," she greeted. "Clear out."

"We've brought you your Thanksgiving dinner," Mrs. Dowdel bellowed at her.

"My what?" old Aunt Madge said. "It ain't even Thanksgiving."

"Yes, it is," Mrs. Dowdel boomed, looming over her.

Aunt Madge squinted up. "From the look of you, it's Halloween."

Mrs. Dowdel wore her flap cap. Aunt Madge wore a floppy straw hat tied under her chins with two mufflers.

"Who are you anyhow?" Her eyes were slits. "You that big gal married Dowdel?"

"That's me," Mrs. Dowdel said. "You want you some chestnut dressing? When did you eat last?"

"I don't know," Aunt Madge said. "What day is it? And who's these two kids? Your grandkids?"

"They might be," Mrs. Dowdel said. "I'll have this boy stick some more cobs in your stove." Meaning me.

"I don't feel the cold," Aunt Madge said. "I'm too old. What's that little gal doin'?" Meaning Ruth Ann.

"She's dishing up some of Wilhelmina Weidenbach's candied yams for you. But you won't like 'em. They're so sweet they'd set your teeth on edge. If you had any."

"Where *is* my teeth?" Aunt Madge wondered, looking around. She spied Dad, pouring out a jar of gravy on the white meat. "Who's that owlhoot?"

"He's the preacher," Mrs. Dowdel bellowed at her.

"What's he here for?"

"I brought him to preach your funeral in case you die before we can get some eats in you."

Ruth Ann stared at that. Dad too.

"I ain't dyin' today," Aunt Madge said. "I'm waitin' for Thanksgiving because they're goin' to bring me my dinner."

Aunt Madge managed to put away a lot of dinner, though she had to gum everything. She wanted seconds on everything except the candied yams. And she wanted a double-wide slice of pie.

We were all watching her eat when a sound from outside made us jump. Dad dashed for the doorway and hit his head. I followed. It was the sound of the Pickle roaring to life. Then the clump of the hood and the bang of a car door. When we looked out, the Pickle was wheeling around in the barnlot, throwing gravel. Now it was gunning down the lane and away in a cloud of exhaust. Dad grabbed for his car keys, and they were in his pocket. Somebody had hotwired our Pickle and stolen it out from under our noses. Dad looked real tense.

Mrs. Dowdel was behind us in the door. "Bagged him," she said. "This time for sure. I figured he'd be needing another car bad, but he won't get far on an eighth of a tank."

She meant Roscoe Burdick. Roscoe Burdick, who'd need wheels because he'd piled up his own car on the Shellabarger steps and sent Phyllis flying. Come to find out, Aunt Madge was Roscoe's grandma.

"I counted on temptation overcoming him if we delivered a car right up to his door." Mrs. Dowdel sounded about half satisfied. Of course, she hadn't told *us* this was where Roscoe Burdick lived.

Dad and I had to tramp back to the Burma-Shave sign on the county road to flag down a ride. In the end, a farmer named Sensenbaugh picked us up and brought us all home. Mrs. Dowdel sat in the cab of the truck with him.

We Barnharts rode in the truck bed behind, wind-whipped all the way back to town. It was really cold back there. Dad held Ruth Ann wrapped in his arms. But she thought it was great, like a hayride, though her eyes streamed and her nose was as red as Aunt Madge's. She wanted to sing "Come, Ye Thankful People, Come," trilling it out across the frosty fields: "All is safely gathered in, e'er the winter storms begin."

CHAPTER THIRTEEN

Selective Service

We got our car back, though it reeked to high heaven of Budweiser and Lucky Strikes, and the ashtray was full. The sheriff of Macon County west of us had pulled Roscoe over on the Lost Bridge road. So Roscoe was in a pickle in more ways than one. The sheriff over there wouldn't hold him but overnight. C. P. Snokes over here didn't want him that long.

Everybody heard, of course. Grounded up in her room, Phyllis heard. Hermits heard. Everybody agreed that Dad wouldn't press charges. With Dad it had to do with turning the other cheek.

But the Macon County sheriff wouldn't set Roscoe loose in his county. C. P. Snokes had to go over and haul him back.

"Bring him directly to my place," Mrs. Dowdel said. And C. P. Snokes did because it was always easier just to do as she said.

She told all us Barnharts to come over too, as quick as we saw the police chief's Dodge pull in. Phyllis too—all of us. Ruth Ann was probably already over there. She and Mrs. Dowdel were getting real serious about fruitcakes and nut bread and divinity fudge.

It was just evening on that Friday after Thanksgiving. The whole town was eating leftovers when the official Dodge turned in at Mrs. Dowdel's, towing our Pickle.

"I don't want Phyllis anywhere near that crooked boy," Mother said. But Mrs. Dowdel had been particular about Phyllis coming too.

Phyllis was looking pale and washed out, but she was anxious to be with Roscoe in what she called "his hour of need," since even the sheriff of Macon County was prejudiced against him.

We trooped over there, under the suet trees, around the Dodge and the Pickle. We went on up to Mrs. Dowdel's front door since this was a formal call. Ruth Ann opened it.

Her apron trailed the floor. Her braids were tied up, and there was flour on her face. "Hoo-boy," she piped, jerking a small thumb behind her. "They've got the jailbird here. Come on in. Wipe your feet."

I was kind of hoping Roscoe would be cuffed, behind his back. After all, he'd sure trussed me up good before he pitched me in the crick. I was still bearing that grudge. I still am.

It was nearly winter, so the parlor stove was up and aglow. I'd never been in Mrs. Dowdel's front room. An old gasolier light fixture hung down. The paper was loose on the walls. Mrs. Dowdel sat in a platform rocker. Her specs reflected red flame from the isinglass window on the stove.

C. P. Snokes and Roscoe stood by. Roscoe was still more or less in custody, but, sadly, not in handcuffs. His sideburns were down to here, and his shirt was unbuttoned down to there. He was gazing away at nothing and chewing something. Maybe gum, maybe not.

At this sight of him, Phyllis made a small squeaking sound. A candied-cherry smell drifted in from the kitchen.

"Doggone it, Mrs. Dowdel," the police chief was saying, "I can't hold him at headquarters overnight without charging him. Anyhow, if I had him to sleep there, he'd dig his way out. You know what these Burdicks is. They're like a passel of chicken-eatin' raccoons. They can burrow in and burrow out of pretty nearly anyplace."

"Well, if you turn him loose, you better sleep in your Dodge," Mrs. Dowdel remarked, "or he'll hotwire it out from under you."

Roscoe shrugged off this whole conversation. His weird blue-and-green gaze drifted Phyllis's way. He seemed to be humming some song just under his breath, and it may have been "Are You Lonesome Tonight?"

Phyllis quivered.

"Mrs. Dowdel," said the police chief, "my hands is tied."

Roscoe's big hands were on his Levi hips. He could hum, chew, and sneer all at the same time.

I personally thought he was a free man already. We all did. We were wrong.

C. P. Snokes glanced over at Dad. "I doubt if the preacher's going to press charges."

"Well," Dad said, "I'm sure the boy is sorry for—"

"Nobody around here presses charges against the Burdicks," Mrs. Dowdel proclaimed. "It's the best way I know of to get your outbuildings burned down under mysterious circumstances."

"Prejudice," Phyllis muttered.

"Hush," Mother said to her.

"Pure prejudice," Phyllis muttered.

C. P. Snokes said, "So my hands is—"

"But you might cast your thoughts back to this galoot's eighteenth birthday," Mrs. Dowdel said. She was smoothing the apron across her mighty knees. Her mouth worked in a thoughtful way as she cast her own thoughts back.

Roscoe himself seemed to think back to whatever he

might have been up to on his eighteenth birthday.

"What did he do?" the police chief asked.

"It's what he didn't do," Mrs. Dowdel replied.

A silence fell over us. The smoke sighed up the stovepipe. Late November wind twanged in the lightning rods above.

"He didn't register with the draft board," Mrs. Dowdel said, "to serve his two years in the army, which is the law. The federal law."

Phyllis had been receding into the shadows. She stopped and swayed slightly. Roscoe hadn't done his army service like . . . Elvis. He was a—what do you call it?

"He's a draft dodger," Mrs. Dowdel said. "They can put him away for that."

I didn't know who to look at, Roscoe or Phyllis.

"Oh well shoot, Mrs. Dowdel," C. P. Snokes said, "I have an idea the army wouldn't want him. Anyhow, the draft board meets over at the county seat. I doubt if any of them citizens on the board ever heard tell of the Burdicks."

"Snokes," Mrs. Dowdel said, "do you know who any of them citizens on the board is?"

"Well, I don't know as I could put a name to any of them. They drafted me in 1940, and all that bunch is dead or out of office."

"I could name you one," Mrs. Dowdel said in a loud, carrying voice.

Then an eerie thing happened.

We were all there in the circle of orange light around the parlor stove, Phyllis over at the edge. But now a figure was there in the door to the kitchen. Small, gnomish, and neckless, but there.

Ruth Ann was all eyes. Who wasn't?

"Come on in, Flora." Mrs. Dowdel waved a hand. And into our midst stepped Miss Flora Shellabarger, Miss Cora's feistier sister.

Roscoe wasn't chewing anything now. He'd swallowed hard.

"Evening, all," Miss Flora said grimly. The same Miss Flora who'd got her front yard plowed under and her mounting block chipped when Roscoe lost control of his DeSoto and Ph—

"Roscoe Burdick," she said, scanning all the way up him, "I've overlooked your case because I didn't want to wish you on the U. S. Army. But I'd be derelict in my duties as chair of the Selective Service Committee if I left you at large another night. Maybe the army can make something out of you. You haven't made anything out of yourself except a public nuisance, a danger to young girls, and a waste of space."

She was a small woman and dried up, and she had no neck to speak of. But she didn't mince words.

Roscoe had pretty poor posture, but he drooped some

more and went pale. Even his sideburns looked worried. He reached for his ear. But he'd smoked his last Lucky Strike.

"You'll be doing a two-year hitch for Uncle Sam, beginning with boot camp," Miss Flora said. "Or you'll be doing two years' hard time in the federal slammer down at Marion. What's it to be? And bear in mind, I speak as a representative of the federal government in Washington, D. C., and the administration of President Dwight D. Eisenhower."

Even I noticed that Phyllis's head was whirling. Her own personal Elvis had been a draft dodger while the real Elvis was serving his country. And looking good in his uniform. Phyllis didn't know what to think, but it was too good a moment to miss. A quick inventory of every Elvis Presley movie seemed to unreel across her brain.

"I'll wait for you, Roscoe," she blurted. "However long. Don't be too . . . shook up."

Mother sighed.

C. P. Snokes was pointing Roscoe at the porch.

"Love me tender," Phyllis called out with a catch in her voice.

Roscoe left on the milk train for the induction center at St. Louis. Miss Flora Shellabarger processed his papers personally. The clerk at the Norfolk & Western depot flagged down the train and gave Roscoe a free ticket for the chair car, donated by a grateful community. C. P. Snokes put him on the train.

Quite a few people stood out on their porches that nippy Saturday morning, gladly seeing Roscoe off. As the train pulled out through town, Mrs. Dowdel herself stood on her front porch, waving Roscoe good-bye with a dish towel in her mighty hand.

CHAPTER FOURTEEN

Season of Secrets and Surprises

On the subject of Christmas Mrs. Dowdel made herself clear. It was just another day as far as she was concerned, and she meant to do very little about it this year.

On the other hand, her Monarch stove hadn't cooled since Thanksgiving. Her kitchen was stacked to the ceiling with black walnut fudge, candied orange peel, Linzertorte, sugar cookies in shapes, pfeffernuss, gingerbread people, springerle, brandy snaps, heavenly hash, popcorn balls, glazed chestnuts, and some fifty pounds of peanut brittle rolled out on a marble top from one of her front room tables. Also, she'd ordered a turkey from the IGA store.

There in front of the IGA the Veterans of Foreign Wars were selling Christmas trees. Mrs. Dowdel was on hand when they opened for business. Several witnesses lingered to observe the rare sight of her shopping for anything. And several reported how she gave each and every tree a good shake to see how dry its needles were. Also, she bad-mouthed several.

A new thing for the Christmas of 1958 was trees sprayed white. One of them was sprayed in a pink that would have shamed Phyllis's bedroom walls. Witnesses reported that Mrs. Dowdel staggered backward in her gum boots when she came to the pink one.

The only tree of any interest to her was a blue spruce nine foot tall. She grabbed it by the neck, shook the living daylights out of it, and seemed to approve. But when she heard they wanted two and a quarter for it, she erupted like Mount Vesuvius. "I only want the one tree," she was heard to thunder, "not the whole grove."

Everybody in town figured she could afford any tree on the lot with what she'd earned off her roadside stand in the time of the Kickapoo Princess. But it hurt Mrs. Dowdel's feelings to spend money. I'd heard her say many a time that she had short arms and long pockets.

When Mr. Milton Grider asked her why she wouldn't settle for a tabletop tree in the seventy-five-cent range, she said she wanted a good big one to fill up her bay window, "to light the way for his coming."

And whether she meant the Christchild or somebody else, no witness knew.

Ruth Ann thought she knew.

We were seeing a little more of Ruth Ann these days. With the Christmas baking behind them, Mrs. Dowdel was shooing her home, sometimes before dark. Mrs. Dowdel was full of secrets. But then Christmas is the season of secrets, and surprises. It sure was around here.

Ruth Ann was somewhat sulky. "Mrs. Dowdel says we better have our chimney swept. And we don't even have a fireplace." Ruth Ann twitched. "And she's going to have a big tree lit up in her bay window to show him the way. She's just trying to pull the wool over my eyes."

Ruth Ann's grown-up front teeth were about halfway in now. She didn't whistle and spit so much when she talked. Mother was grooming her for a solo in the choir concert.

"Why do you think Mrs. Dowdel is trying to pull the wool over your eyes?" Dad asked.

Ruth Ann slumped. "She thinks I'm nothing but a little kid. I'm practically halfway through first grade, and she don't even notice."

"She doesn't even notice," Mother corrected.

"You can say that again," Ruth Ann said. "She thinks I'm worried he'll be looking for me in Terre Haute, not here."

It was just the four of us at the table. Phyllis was upstairs writing a letter to either Elvis or Roscoe.

"Who, honey?" Dad said.

"You know who, Daddy. S-A-N-T-A," Ruth Ann spelled, "C-L-A-U-S."

The kitchen clock ticked loud in the silence.

"I haven't believed since the first month of school."

She drew up her small shoulders to shrug off Santa Claus. "Word gets around."

Mother and Dad looked a little sorry. Ruth Ann had been the last Santa believer among us, and now—

"But, honey, are you sure?" Dad said. "What about leaving out cookies for Santa's treat?"

"Daddy, you ate the cookies."

"What about . . . reindeer on the roof?"

"Please, Daddy. How would they get up there?"

"Honey, don't you want to hang up your stocking on Christmas Eve?" It was Dad's last offer. Ruth Ann pondered.

She pulled on more chins than she had. She really was a miniature Mrs. Dowdel. At least with her teeth coming in, she looked a little less like Mrs. Wilcox. "I hadn't thought about the stocking," she said. "But I'm not a baby anymore." She poked invisible specs back up her nose. "In many important ways I'm practically ten."

But Grachel was there in her lap. Without the doll buggy, Grachel never got out now. But she rarely missed a meal. Ruth Ann was holding her up so she could look one-eyed across the oilcloth and see everything.

As it turned out, Mrs. Dowdel got her Christmas tree, and it didn't cost her a thin dime. It could have cost her her life, and me mine. But it was a free tree.

Christmas was on a Thursday that year, and two Saturdays

before it, I was doing some chores for Mrs. Dowdel. She could round you up, cut you out of the herd, and throw a harness on you before you knew it. She wasn't working Ruth Ann that Saturday because Ruth Ann was at church with Mother, rehearsing for the Christmas Eve choir concert. So was Phyllis. She had to be in the choir too and didn't like it, mainly because Ruth Ann had the solo.

Anyway, it was in the middle of that Saturday morning, and I thought it was time for a break and maybe a slice of fruitcake. Mrs. Dowdel had baked a gross of them. We'd been working hard. She'd turned all the mattresses, aired the sheets, beat the rugs. I'd had a raft of stuff to bring down from the attic. We were busy as bird dogs. In fact, we were up to something.

Instead of the fruitcake, she said, "Go on out to the cobhouse and find that coil of rope. Bring the biggest saw."

I should have seen what was coming right there.

When I came out of the cobhouse, she was on her back porch, dressed in her full outdoor gear: flap cap, hunting jacket, two wash dresses and an apron over a pair of men's pants, cotton stockings over her sleeves, railroader's gloves. Gum boots. She was everything but armed.

"Where's your paw?" she inquired, gazing elsewhere.

I told her Dad was working at the food distribution center. All the same people we'd fed at Thanksgiving would be needing Christmas dinners.

"Where's your car keys?"

I stared up at her. Surely she didn't know how to drive a car. Except for Mrs. Weidenbach, the only old woman in town who drove was Miss Flora Shellabarger. She had a 1942 Packard Clipper, and she was all over the road with it.

"Above the visor on the driver's side," I said.

"Well, we'll naturally have to take the car," she said, businesslike. "How else are we going to get to the timber for a tree? Hoo-boy, here comes Effie."

Sure enough here came Mrs. Wilcox across the yard in her usual rig: Mackinaw jacket, veiled hat, carpet slippers. And today, yarn mittens. "She always knows when I'm goin' anywhere. I'd have to chloroform her and tie her down to get away without her."

"I just happened to be passin'," Mrs. Wilcox sang out. She'd swerved off the road to open country.

The three of us tramped across the yards to where the Pickle was parked. A little pale morning sun had cleared the frost off the windshield, and the first light snow of the season.

None of this seemed quite right.

But when I'd thrown the rope and a big two-handled crosscut saw into the trunk, they were both in the car already. Mrs. Wilcox was in the back. Mrs. Dowdel was on the front seat.

But not behind the wheel.

"I'll ride shotgun," she said when I opened the driver's-side door. I couldn't see a moment ahead. She was hunkered down and staring straight out through the windshield. "You drive."

"Mrs. Dowdel, I don't have a driver's license. I'm only—"

"A license?" She could hardly believe her ears. "We're not goin' out on Route 36. We're just goin' country roads."

"But—"

"And you're long enough in the leg," she observed. "You've growed an inch and a half just here this fall."

"An inch and five-eighths," I muttered.

"Well then, you'll reach the pedals, easy."

"I don't know how to drive." But my knee was on the seat. My hand closed over the steering wheel. I thought it'd be another four long years before I could drive. Three and a half to a learner's permit. Forty-two months. I'd dreamed of the day. But it was a distant dream.

"You've watched your paw drive many a time," Mrs. Dowdel said. "If men can drive a car, how much can there be to it?"

"Hoo-boy," Mrs. Wilcox said softly from behind.

I was behind the wheel now. One hand gripped it.

The other reached up for the keys. My heart was pounding like pistons. I adjusted the rearview mirror. I knew where the key went. I knew where the starter was. I knew you started in neutral. I hit the starter.

In cold weather the Pickle was usually balky as a mule. It

started right up and roared. I watched my hand go for the gearshift. I yanked it into a gear. Maybe first gear. The Pickle howled in pain. I jammed a sneaker down on the clutch and tried again. The Pickle took a giant leap, and died.

"Hold her!" Mrs. Dowdel called out from up against the glove box. "She's rarin'!"

Mrs. Wilcox disappeared completely from the rearview mirror.

My heart was in my mouth, but my sneaker was on the clutch. I hit the starter, eased into a gear. By chance my sneaker found the gas. We moved. Mrs. Wilcox reappeared in the mirror with her hat on sideways.

The first leap had nearly taken out the grape arbor. But now I tried to steer because we were aimed at the back porch. The steering on a 1950 Nash is loose as a goose, and the hood's as big as an aircraft carrier. But we lumbered around the arbor and along the side of our house. We were still on private property, but the street was right there at the end of the hood.

"Find the brake," Mrs. Dowdel mentioned.

There were two of them, the hand brake and the pedal that wasn't the clutch. I used both. We skidded to a stop. My head hit the steering wheel and honked the horn.

"Go left," Mrs. Dowdel advised. "We don't want to drive through town."

I gave it a little gas, and we leaped out on the snowy slab

like a jack rabbit. Did I look both ways? But nothing was coming.

We surged along in giant jerks. Mrs. Wilcox was all over the backseat. Another gear. Where was it? I remembered about the clutch. We whined into second.

I was right there on the crown of the road. If we'd met anything coming at us, I wouldn't be here to tell you about it. "Pick a side," Mrs. Dowdel said.

I swerved to the ditch and back into the right lane. Mrs. Wilcox seemed to be holding on to a back door handle with both hands. Mrs. Dowdel rode shotgun with her knees wide and her boots planted. Open country unfolded ahead. I discovered third gear, and the whole day brightened.

I went left when I was told, and I went right when I was told. Every turn took me on a big sweep across both lanes with the fender swooping out over the ditch. But we made it. I was breathing pretty even now, though my heart still hammered. It was like the first day of my life. We edged up to thirty miles an hour. The fences flickered past. Cattle out in the fields stood broadside to the sun. Smoke rose from farmhouse chimneys. I still wasn't thinking ahead. I couldn't chance it. But there for a while on the straight stretch I wasn't even a kid.

I was sixteen.

Since I couldn't see over the steering wheel, I had to see through it. Now a scary sight loomed ahead. A big bean truck was coming our way, taking more than his share. Mrs.

Dowdel's shoulder came up, but she didn't say anything.

"Hoo," said Mrs. Wilcox, and I shot off the road to give the bean truck all the room there was. But it was shoulder, not ditch. We threw gravel and bounced hard, but I got us swerved back and bumped up on the hardtop.

Now there was timber on both sides. We were coming up on a bridge over Salt Crick. I had to line up the wheels with the boards of the bridge, and I made it onto one of them. We clattered across into deeper timber.

"Pull off where you see that track."

I geared down for the turn. We made it between a pair of fence posts, but it was close. I listened for the sound of peeling chrome.

It wasn't even a track after a while. It was just brush and snow in the ruts. When we were out of sight of the road, Mrs. Dowdel said, "Wheel around and pull up." I turned in a clearing, and the engine coughed, lunged, and died. I was wringing wet and about as happy as I'd ever been.

Mrs. Dowdel swung open her door and began to fight her way out. "Get the saw," she told me. Then she looked in the backseat. "And you stay in the car, Effie. It's rough underfoot, and if you broke a leg, we'd have to shoot you."

Through bare branches we saw a stand of evergreens. I supposed Mrs. Dowdel knew exactly where they were. She tramped through the underbrush and over fallen logs. It was colder and quieter than the rest of outdoors. Winter birds watched us from high branches. Mrs. Dowdel stopped just to drink it all in. She always thought the town was too loud and crowded. But the two moons of her specs were already spotting for trees.

She moved among them, looking over the long-needled pine and the blue spruce, overlooking the scrawny ones.

The saw was heavy in my hand. She took her time, but then she said, "There it is."

It was a tall blue spruce, taller than we could use, but we could cut it to the right length. She took one end of the saw, and I took the other. In the last moment before we started, she listened to the silence. Then we began to saw.

It was all I could do to keep up my end. She was like a buzz saw herself. In no time at all, the tree began to topple, and she pushed the oozing trunk away.

Between us, we began to drag it back to the Pickle. Just at the edge of the clearing was about a six-foot tree with a perfect cone shape.

"That one do for you folks?"

So we cut that one too. Mrs. Wilcox was all eyes from the backseat. Between us we got both trees roped to the roof of the car. I wasn't a lot of help with that part, but Mrs. Dowdel could reach halfway across the top.

I thought we were done, but she said, "We'll need us some greens for wreaths."

So back we trekked. She'd brought a folding knife. We

worked farther into the trees, looking for the right branches, full and feathery. She cut, I carried.

Then she went too far. She'd pushed past one last fir tree, stopped dead, and staggered back. I almost walked up the back of her gum boots.

There ahead of us past freshly laid sod was a brand-new house, ranch style with attached garage and picture window. Even a bird feeder. We were standing in somebody's back-yard.

"Where in the Sam Hill did that place come from?" she wondered. You rarely saw her astonished, but she was. We thought we'd been out in the middle of nowhere. I heard voices, a door, the scrape of feet.

She spun around and nearly knocked me flat. "Run for your life," she said. "Don't drop the greens."

We plunged, skimming the undergrowth, clearing logs. She had the saw. Gunfire behind us would have come as no surprise. Neither would snarling dogs. I ran like a blind boy with my face in the feathery greens. To this day the smell of fir and pine brings back that morning.

Back at the car it was all a blur. Somehow the trunk lid was down, and Mrs. Dowdel and I were in the front seat, fighting for breath.

"Lay rubber," she said.

"Where's the fire?" Mrs. Wilcox said.

Then she vanished out of my rearview mirror because I

found first gear with no trouble. The Pickle rocketed down the track. I aimed between the fence posts and screeched out on the road on two wheels. Once again if something had been coming, I wouldn't be telling this.

We headed back the way we'd come, top-heavy with trees. I was working through the gears like a pro now, and Mrs. Dowdel was wiping up under her specs with a blue bandanna. "Hoo-boy," she said. "Busy, busy, busy and rushed off my feet. Not enough hours in the day. I'll die standing up like an old—"

"Ox," Mrs. Wilcox said from behind. "Did you see anything of the Dempseys?"

"Who in tarnation are the Dempseys?" Mrs. Dowdel asked.

"Why, they's the folks who bought up that whole tract of land and put up a new house on it."

My eyes were mostly on the road, but I noticed Mrs. Dowdel's fists clench on her knees.

"Many thanks for sharin' that news, Effie," she said in a dangerous voice.

And we drove on back to town.

I did.

CHAPTER FIFTEEN

The Gift

Since Christmas is also the season of miracles, we were back before we were missed. On the last lap, I got a little overconfident the way you do at twelve. I needed more work on my steering and nearly took out Mrs. Dowdel's mailbox. But then we were creeping back past our house. I managed to park the Pickle in its regular ruts. It lurched one last time, and the engine died. I put the keys back where they belonged.

Maybe Mother and Dad thought the tree that turned up in our front room was Mrs. Dowdel's payment for chores I'd been doing for her. Maybe they thought that both that tree and the big one that filled Mrs. Dowdel's bay window had come from the VFW tree sale up at the IGA. Maybe I let them think it.

Mrs. Dowdel and Ruth Ann decorated for days. They gilded pinecones and strung enough popcorn for two trees. The first graders made paper chains at school, and Ruth Ann made extra. The tree in the bay to show him the way glowed like Times Square with strand after strand of fat-bulbed lights.

There were no presents under Mrs. Dowdel's tree though. She said she didn't give any because of inflation.

There was a tree in every front window in town, against the blue glow of television sets. And a wreath on every door. A full-size beaverboard nativity scene, floodlit, appeared in the park uptown where Gypsy Piggott's big top had stood last summer. Woody's Zephyr Oil filling station gave out inflatable plastic snowmen with every lube job.

And night after night the strains of a heavenly host singing al-le-lu-ia welled out of our church as Mother rehearsed the concert choir.

Actual heavenly hosts looking down on the town could have taken it for the toy village under a Christmas tree, complete with train track and winking lights. A light dusting of snow on Christmas Eve was the final touch.

The town bustled now with company coming: kids home from college, soldiers on leave. Company for Christmas.

After a sketchy supper at our house, the bustle turned to panic. Mother said the Christmas choir concert was her first opportunity to share Methodist music with what she called

The Larger Community. She was worried sick they didn't have all the bugs out of "Ring Out Wild Bells." Then she couldn't find her pitch pipe.

The Methodist women had made Christmas choir robes out of army surplus sheeting. Phyllis said she looked like Casper the Ghost in hers. She and Mother had given each other Toni home permanents, but this hadn't calmed them. Ruth Ann's choir robe was a mile too long. She kept tripping over it and stumbling into things. She was sure she had her solo down pat. Mother wasn't.

The house vibrated with women. They were in and out of every room. You couldn't hear yourself think. And the concert was still an hour off. Dad and I got our coats and went outside, but it was too cold on the porch. We went around back and sat in the Pickle to be out of the wind. Dad had on his old pea coat from the navy, over his robe with the velvet. He hadn't worn it since the princess's funeral.

As soon as we were in the car, I knew it wasn't a good idea. There was a heavy evergreen smell and pine needles everywhere. For some reason.

We had a clear view of Mrs. Dowdel's house. Lights were on upstairs and down. The kitchen glowed like a blazing pumpkin with last-minute cooking. She'd sent Ruth Ann home way before dark, and she'd been seen down at the depot, waiting for somebody off the train.

"She has a fine tree," Dad remarked, brushing pine needles off the Pickle's dashboard.

To change the subject, I said, "But there aren't any presents under it. She doesn't give gifts."

One of Dad's hands rested on the steering wheel, there in the dark. "You sure about that?"

I thought I was. "She mentioned inflation."

"Maybe she doesn't wait for Christmas. Have you had a gift from her already?"

"You don't mean anything wrapped up with ribbon, right?" I said.

"No," Dad said. "Nothing that small."

I thought. But I couldn't get past the day she'd told me to drive the Pickle. That was a great day. Every night since, I'd dreamed myself back to it. In my dreams I was behind the wheel, gearing down, double-clutching. And there was never oncoming traffic, and I was always in the right gear. I drove with one elbow out of the window in my dreams. And I was sixteen and six foot tall. With shoulders out to here. And nobody, but nobody was going to tie me up and pitch me in the crick. Let them try.

Dad sat there, giving me some time. You could see our breath. The glow from Mrs. Dowdel's tree spilled out of her bay across the white yard like a welcome mat.

"Dad, who's that tree lighting the way for? Mrs. Dowdel didn't mean the Christchild, did she?"

"No," Dad said. "The Christchild's been there all year long."

A moment passed, pine-scented. "Then who?"

Dad stirred, reached for the door handle. "Somebody

we're just about to meet. And he's due now. We'd better get in the house to make him welcome."

I was stumped. "To our house?"

Dad nodded. "A visitor from afar."

"You mean like one of the three Wise Men?" I was as lost as usual.

"Not exactly," Dad said. "But he'll probably be bearing a gift."

We headed up to the house then. Dad's hand was on my shoulder, which I liked.

"And son," he said, "when you get a minute, take that crosscut saw out of the Pickle's trunk and put it back in Mrs. Dowdel's cobhouse."

CHAPTER SIXTEEN

A Christmas Wedding

In the house the countdown to Christmas was ticking like a time bomb. Mother had found her pitch pipe, but her sheet music was out of order. They'd pinned up Ruth Ann's robe. Phyllis was at a mirror, biting her lips to make them pinker. Dad and I hadn't been missed.

A knock came at the front door.

Ruth Ann began to turn to it. Dad's hand came out to hold her back. Mother never looked up from her sheet music. She made sure Phyllis had to answer the door.

A boy was standing out there with something in his hand. It looked like a cellophane-covered brick, tied up in Christmas tinsel. He took one look at Phyllis, and his eyes bugged slightly. Evidently she didn't look too much like Casper the Ghost. She may have seemed like an angel in all that white, if you didn't know her.

"Hello. I'm Brad Dowdel. Mrs. Dowdel's great-grandson. Joey's son." His voice had already changed. "Here for the holidays."

Phyllis made a small squeaking sound. It took her a while, but she got out of his way so he could come in. Ruth Ann's eyes were saucers. He was one good-looking dude of a boy. Blond-headed. And he was wearing a bomber jacket with some fine Levi's and white buck shoes. No sideburns, yet. But come to find out, he was just fourteen, Phyllis's age. Her real age.

And very polite for a Chicago guy. We all introduced ourselves, and he handed Mother the present, which was a fruitcake.

"There's more where that came from," he said. "Great-grandma thought I might go on up to the Christmas concert with you folks."

"I expect she'll be along later," Mother said.

But I wondered, since Mrs. Dowdel wasn't a church woman. Still, I was beginning to figure out that adults move in mysterious ways.

"Phyllis will be up in the choir loft," Mother told Brad. "And of course Ruth Ann. But you can help Bob usher."

So as Dad predicted, we did have a visitor from afar— Chicago. He was even bearing a gift, if you count fruit-cake.

Brad Dowdel and I had our hands full finding everybody

a place to sit. Finally people were standing at the back. It wasn't quite the overflow crowd we'd had for the princess's funeral, but it was getting there.

As Mother said, we were making a joyful noise for the larger community. There were people there you wouldn't expect. Not Miss Cora Shellabarger. But then, she'd been spotted off her porch only twice since before the Korean Police Action. But I myself showed Miss Flora to a pew.

Everybody noticed everybody else. As the pews filled, a murmur swept the congregation. People craned to look back to a disturbance at the door.

Barging in were four or maybe five of the roughest characters I ever saw. Not a haircut among them and only about six teeth. They were bundled up against the winter night in a raggedy combination of caked army surplus and dirty denim. All wore farmer caps, and all were chewing something. As the saying went around here, hogs wouldn't have stayed on their place. One or two of them may have been women.

A whispered name fanned like a breeze across the pews: "Burdicks."

Just in case Brad and I thought we were going to show them to a pew, one of them put out a big banged-up hand, meaning "back off."

And in they ganged, sticking close. They were carrying something, a bundle in their midst. People in the back pew scooted over to make room for them. Way over. There in the pew the bundle they'd brought stirred. And sat up. One minute it was a pile of rags with an old floppy hat on top. The next minute it was Aunt Madge. Aunt Madge Burdick.

She glared around at the crowd, who were all staring back. There must have been plenty of people here who hadn't seen her in this century.

"Are they goin' to give me any supper?" she demanded in a high, cracked voice. "Where *is* my teeth?"

We heard singing from outside then, not a moment too soon. I switched off the lights. Voices rose from out on the sidewalk, "O come, all ye faithful, joyful and triumphant . . . " The choir proceeded inside, two by two, carrying candles. It was a choir twice the Sunday size.

O come let us adore Him, O come let us adore Him,
they sang, all the way up to the choir loft.

The VFW had donated all their unsold trees, so the choir gathered in front of a somewhat scrubby pine forest.

Last in the procession came Dad in his robe. And holding his hand, Ruth Ann, who looked like the littlest angel, at least for this evening.

Dad ascended the pulpit, though he did very little preaching from up there. Ruth Ann hiked her robe and took giant steps up into the choir loft, between Mother and Phyllis.

Dad spoke out:

"Let us go to Bethlehem and see this thing that has happened."

An old, cracked voice called out from the back pew, "Luke. 2:15!"

It was Aunt Madge Burdick.

"Ring Out Wild Bells," the choir sang, under Mother's direction. And then "O Holy Night!" Phyllis kept losing her place from glancing up for a glimpse of Brad Dowdel, out here in the dark.

Dad followed up by reading the Christmas story, the one that begins: "Now there were in the same country shepherds living out in the fields, keeping watch over their flocks by night . . ."

"Luke," Aunt Madge crackled out from the back, "every bit of it!"

The choir sang all the carols in the hymnal, and then it was time for Ruth Ann. Mother gave her a little boost forward, and Ruth Ann raised her candle.

"Sing out, honey," Mother was heard to murmur, and Ruth Ann began,

"Away in a manger, no crib for a bed,
The little Lord Jesus laid down His sweet head . . ."

Everybody in the flickering room listened with both ears as Ruth Ann worked through the stanzas to

"Bless all the dear children in Thy tender care,
And fit us for heaven, to live with Thee there."

She had it down pat.

Then it was nearly over, or so we thought. Dad stood to give us a benediction:

> *While shepherds watch their flocks by night,*
> *We're gathered here by candlelight;*
> *Snug we are and manger-warm,*
> *Against the winds of winter storm.*
> *Gathered behind these windows stout*
> *That keep December's fury out,*
> *Gather we here from near and far*
> *To wait with the world for a glimpse of the star.*

Aunt Madge's old crooked finger came up in the dark, but she drew it back. This may not have been Scripture. It may have come straight from Dad.

The choir rustled their robes, getting ready to proceed out. They shuffled their sheet music to "As with Gladness Men of Old."

Then everything changed. Brad and I were at the back, flanking the door when it banged open. Wind blew in. Candles blew out. People jumped. Brad and I fell back. An enormous figure filled the door—bear big. "Hit the lights," it said.

So I did. The church flooded with electric light, and it was Mrs. Dowdel there in the door. Her hunting jacket was over an arm, but she was dressed as I'd never seen her.

It must have been her good dress. Maroon with a lot of tucks or whatever across her massive front. Big black shiny shoes too. The bun on the back of her head rode high, with combs. She was . . . all dolled up.

The choir hung in the loft. Mother had put up a hand to hold them there. Why did I have the sudden suspicion that she and Mrs. Dowdel were working as a team again?

I had a vague vision of Mother with that Winchester broken open over her arm. But the front pew people were on their feet, looking back. Mrs. Dowdel's name swept the room.

"Hold it right there, Preacher!" she hollered out to Dad. "We've got us another item of business in the presence of these witnesses."

People gawked at each other. Who did she think she was, busting up a choir concert? She wasn't even a church woman. And what business?

But Dad didn't look too surprised. In fact he looked glad to see her. Delighted even. He beamed. "And what is that business, Mrs. Dowdel?" he called back to her.

"A wedding," she said. The room buzzed like a hive. "A Christmas wedding."

"Marriage is a sacrament, Mrs. Dowdel, as you know," Dad remarked. "But it is also a legal contract, and we'll need to see—"

"The marriage license," she boomed. "I got it right here."

She reached down the front of her dress and drew out the marriage license. She could have kept the entire Bill of Rights down there.

"The bride's not of age," she called out, "but her mother's signed off on her. She don't have much choice."

"Without further explanation, Mrs. Dowdel," Dad said, "let us have the happy couple come forth."

Mrs. Dowdel lumbered aside and waved them in.

A couple stepped up. I was as close to them as I am to you, and it was the surprise of my young life. At first, I thought it was Elvis Presley come among us. I wasn't the only one. The room gasped. But it wasn't Elvis.

It was Roscoe Burdick with a GI haircut and a close shave in the dress uniform of a U.S. Army private: the full pinks and greens, and spit-shined shoes. Necktie and all. A necktie on a Burdick was a sight to behold, though Roscoe was swallowing hard. It was Roscoe home on special leave from Basic Training at Fort Leonard Wood.

Beside him, her hair ablaze in the night, was Waynetta Blalock in the same outfit she'd worn on the homecoming queen's parade float. It didn't fit her as well now. Her dress-up suit strained around her middle. But she had a good firm grip on Roscoe. She'd always said she could make something out of him, Burdick or not.

As the Sunday *Piatt County Call* newspaper reported, "The bride was attended by her bridesmaids, schoolmates all, Miss Barbara Jean Jeeter, Miss Edna-Earl Stubbs, Miss Vanette Pankey, Miss Bonnie Burhoops, all of this village and each carrying a nosegay of flowers in seasonal colors."

Waynetta was the first high school senior to be married, except for those who'd run off, so that was some satisfaction to her.

It was a satisfaction to Mother too. I happened to notice her up in the choir loft, and I think I read her lips:

   A-le-lu-ia,

they seemed to say. This was by far Mother's best Christmas present: Roscoe Burdick not only in the army, but tied tight in the bonds of matrimony. The first Burdick ever married, in fact.

It was the best present Phyllis ever got too, whether she knew it or not. I couldn't tell from back here. But she seemed to be above it all up there, lofty in the choir loft. If she was having any thoughts at all, they were bound to be about Brad Dowdel.

What Brad made of this sudden wedding I didn't know.

But he was a Chicago guy, so he'd probably seen everything. Besides, he was staying with Mrs. Dowdel, where the whole business must have been cooked up.

Dad pointed to Roscoe and summoned him down to the front. Every eye followed. Roscoe—Private Burdick—turned and gazed back over us. His posture was improved, but there was panic in his blue-and-green stare. Blind panic. Dad nodded to Waynetta.

We had no piano, let alone an organ, and the Wedding March isn't a choral number. Mother had the choir go straight into "Joy to the World."

Though afterward, long after, I overheard her tell Dad that "Lo! How a Rose E'er Blooming" might have been more appropriate. Or even "For Unto Us a Child is Born."

Waynetta teetered down the aisle in her high heels, trailed by her Iota Nu Beta sorority sisters. Mrs. Dowdel herself came next. And behind her for some reason, Mrs. Wilcox in her Mackinaw and veiled hat and carpet slippers.

What her part in the plot was nobody knew. Except she was always all over Mrs. Dowdel like a rubber girdle in a heatwave. You'd have to chloroform her and tie her down to leave her behind.

Several members of the DAR made room for them on the front pew, as Dad began, "Dearly beloved, we are gathered here . . ."

When he came to "Who gives this woman to this man in holy matrimony?" Mrs. Dowdel waved a big hand and called out, "That'd be me, as her maw's at home with a sick headache."

By now the whole congregation was having a whale of a good time. People said later that it was the best Christmas choir concert ever held in Piatt County.

A terrible old cawing voice called out from the back, "And I give the groom!" It was his grandmother, Aunt Madge.

"So do I," called out Miss Flora Shellabarger, waving from the third pew. By now the whole church was practically rolling in the aisles. Waynetta and Roscoe were united in matrimony on wave upon wave of laughter.

But as Dad said afterward, that's not the worst beginning for a young couple embarking upon the choppy seas of the uncertain future.

CHAPTER SEVENTEEN

A Visit from Saint Nick

It was nearly Christmas Day by the time we Barnharts left church. The bride and groom had long fled. What they drove I never knew. The rest of the Burdicks had hauled Aunt Madge back to the sticks. Brad went off between Mrs. Dowdel and Mrs. Wilcox. Miss Flora Shellabarger had fired up her Packard Clipper. But plenty of people wanted to linger on the church steps, replaying the evening and giving one another the greetings of the season.

Dad and I made a final check of all the windows before he locked up the church. It was long afterward before I learned where we came by these top-of-the-line windows stout enough to keep December's fury out.

They'd been paid for with Mrs. Dowdel's profits from her roadside stand back at the time of the Kickapoo

Princess. So she hadn't buried her money in Joey's room or out in the melon patch. She'd given it to the church, though she wasn't a church woman. All her gifts were supposed to be secrets, of course. But it took the whole town to keep a secret.

Ruth Ann was half asleep in Dad's arms as we turned toward home. The big tree still blazing in Mrs. Dowdel's bay window showed us the way, though she'd put it there to show Brad his. Our own tree winked out of the front window across the porch.

As soon as we were inside, we saw we'd had a visitor. There on an end table was a plate of Christmas cookies, half eaten—sugar cookies in shapes and divinity fudge.

Ruth Ann was bolt awake now and sliding down Dad. She rolled her eyes at the cookies and stared at the tree. Actually, the Dempseys' tree.

In front of it stood a doll buggy, and it hadn't come from the Goodwill store. This was an old-timer, tall and wicker with wire wheels and a patent-leather seat. It looked a lot like one Mrs. Dowdel had me bring down from her attic. You could find anything up in that attic.

Now it was freshly sprayed a snowy white with ribbons worked through the wicker. Somehow Grachel had found her way downstairs and into it. She sat in the patent-leather seat, gazing one-eyed around the room, wondering what had kept us.

"Would you look at that," Dad said. "Seems like we've had a visit from Saint Nick while we—"

"Daddy," Ruth Ann said, small but sure, "there is no Santa. Word gets around." But she couldn't take her eyes off that grand, antique doll buggy. She was ready to take Grachel for a midnight airing this minute. She looked up at Phyllis and me like we ought to get ready to go.

"If it wasn't Santa," Dad said, "who was it?"

We waited. Mother's hand slipped into Dad's.

"Hoo-boy," Ruth Ann said. "It was Mrs. Dowdel."

"Was it?" Dad said. "Then I wonder what you could give her in return. Something she'd like. Seems like she's always the one giving the gifts."

Ruth Ann thought. She pulled on more chins than she had. She patted her back hair, braided with white bows to match her choir robe.

"I know what." She raised a small finger. "I could tell her I thought Santa brought it."

"Good girl," Dad said.

Then we all hung up our stockings with care because we did that every year. I hadn't expected much out of this particular Christmas since I was in kind of an in-between time: too old for toys and still forty-two months from a learner's permit. But it was the Christmas we always remembered.

By the time I got up to my room, Mrs. Dowdel had

doused her Christmas tree lights. She'd lit our way home, and she had her great-grandson with her. I expect he was all the Christmas she needed. Her whole house seemed to be asleep, the last house in town. And the melon patch behind. The town slept now, nestled among the silvered fields.

Under a Christmas star.

Epilogue

It was to be our only Christmas in that town, the Christmas of 1958 all those Christmases ago. In another year we were in Quincy, and Dad had the pulpit of Grace Methodist there. By the time I graduated from high school, we were in Rockford. Phyllis was at Illinois Wesleyan University. And Ruth Ann was in junior high, with her own room and a Beatles poster on every wall. You think growing up takes forever, but it doesn't.

Each of Dad's churches was bigger, in a bigger town. From that time when Gypsy Piggott had to fold his revival tent after the first night, Dad's star began to rise. He was especially praised for his funerals and weddings. Word gets around.

We did some growing up wherever we were, but we grew up the most in that little podunk town when we lived next door to Mrs. Dowdel.

She was no church woman, and she didn't neighbor, and Christmas was just another day to her. But she didn't wait for Christmas to give out her gifts. She gave too many. They wouldn't have fit under the tree, not even the tallest blue spruce from the Dempseys' backyard.